I0604469

I WILL FIND YOU

CLUES

- blunt trauma to head
- ~~no murder weapon found~~
- forced entry
- no pants
- voicemail: 'I've been thinking a lot about Regulus'

A DARK HOLE DARKLY

A DETECTIVE'S STORY

BY DREW MELBOURNE

RUESDAY BOOKS

The novel that you're about to read is a work of fiction. By definition, yeah? The individuals, organizations, and events depicted throughout are either wholly fictional or presented in a fictitious manner.

Otherwise, I dunno. I guess this is a more or less a true story?

Copyright © 2025 by Drew Melbourne. All rights reserved.

Visit the author's website at **drewmelbourne.com**.

Published by Ruesday Books.

Paperback ISBN 978-0-9998748-4-4
eBook ISBN 978-0-9998748-5-1

FIRST PAPERBACK EDITION

10 9 8 7 6 5 4 3 2 1

For Mom
and all the stories
never written down

what was

1

what is

91

what should be

189

WHAT WAS

ONE

My girlfriend says I don't have the temperament to solve my mom's murder. And she's right probably. It's been six months, and I haven't done shit.

No. That's not right. I bought a journal. This one. That day. Or. Well, the day after. It was past midnight when I left the crime scene. Walked the four blocks to that CVS. They had a few different ones. Unicorns. Cats. One cat-unicorn. A… unicat, maybe?

Not important.

I picked a plain black one, pebbled, not too big, lined pages, with a strap to keep it closed. It had a nice snap to it, I thought. Satisfying twang. I've written in it three times. First, that night, I took a pen and I wrote in big block letters on the first page:

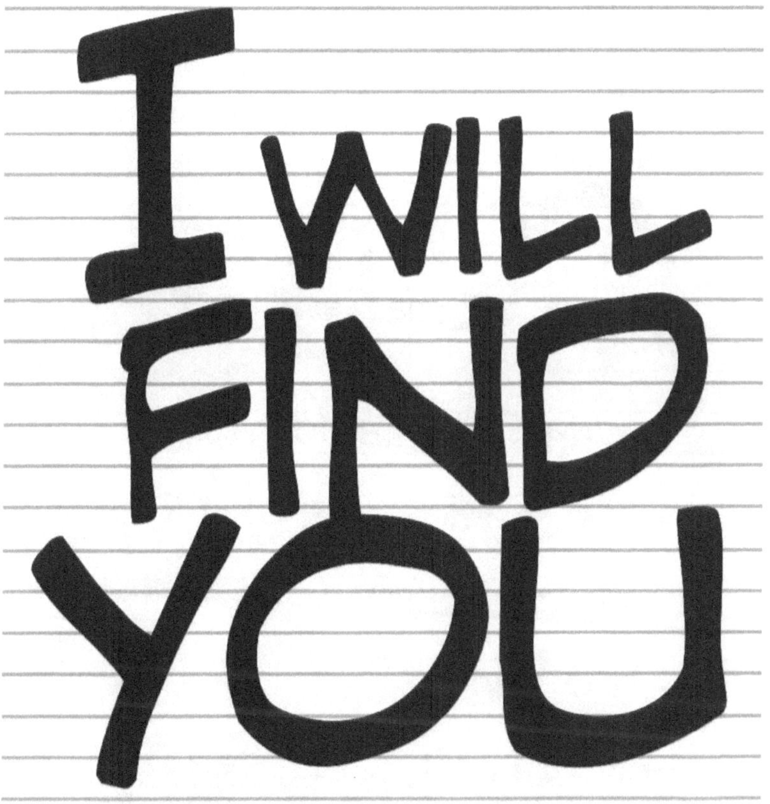

Closed the book. Left it there on the ironing board. Set the pen on top.

Stared for a minute. Deep breath.

Went and found my game controller. Played *Elder Scrolls Online* till five in the morning. Ran three Undaunted quests and leveled my companion to fourteen. Spent the rest of the night redecorating my house.

My in-game house.

Two days later, I picked up the pen, picked up the journal, and I wrote:

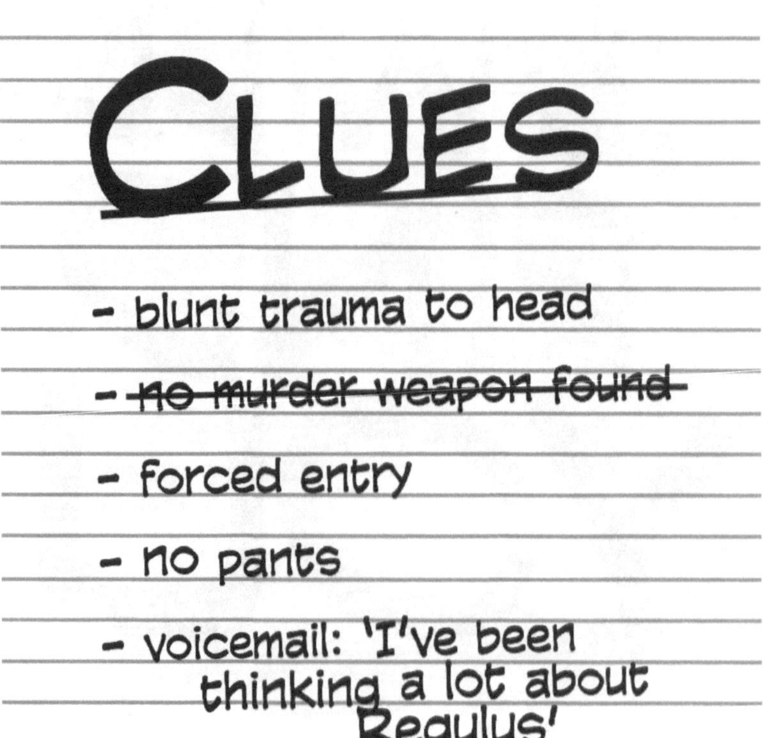

It wasn't much to go on.

I crossed out 'no murder weapon found' because the lack of something can't be a clue. Looking back, I guess 'no pants' is also the lack of something. (Pants.) But it seemed relevant.

She had underwear on. She wasn't

She'd called the night before. That night. I didn't answer. I have trouble with my ringer. Either I don't hear it at all or I crank it and it's too loud and my girlfriend tells me to turn it down again.

She left a forty-seven second message. Mostly silence. At the thirty-two second mark she said in this quiet almost-singsong almost-childlike voice, 'I've been thinking a lot about Regulus.' Then she waited a few more seconds, and then she hung up.

I didn't find the message till after the cops called. I didn't tell them. Didn't want them to confiscate my phone. Didn't want them to take away my mom's last words to me.

When my girlfriend found out a few weeks later she was livid. But that's Lilly. Livid Lilly. Living with livid Lilly. Everything I do is wrong, but never so wrong as when I'm in close, prolonged proximity to other people.

It was a bad fight. It ended when I deleted the voicemail in front of her. Out of spite, obviously. I slept on the bathroom floor that night. In the morning, she stood in the doorway, naked in her disapproval. Disapproving in her nakedness. And she asked, 'What is wrong with you?'

Fuck if I know.

Regulus is a star. One of the brightest. It's Latin for 'little king.' A kinda bird. A kinda horse. A British TV show from the 1980s. A *Bomberman* villain. A kinda rock. A smelting process. A kinda boat. Etc. Etc.

I'm not smart. I just know how to read a Wikipedia disambiguation page.

I asked the detective about the time of death. She said sometime between ten and midnight. Those mighta been her final words: 'I've been thinking a lot about Regulus.' Why though? What the fuck was she trying to tell me?

Was it a message? Was she trying to tell me who killed her?

I didn't know what it meant then.

I do now.

TWO

I met Lilly on line. That's a joke I tell people. She thought it was funny the first two times, and then she asked me to please knock it off.

We were, she will clarify, *in* a line. A very, very, very long line. Barnes & Noble on Union Square. Good location: 4, 5, 6, L, N, R, Q, W. An author was there to sign books and, hopefully, a few of my dad's old comics. The line went down the stairs, out the front door, and around the block. I was there on my lunch hour. And also for a good chunk of the afternoon. Thankfully I have one of those jobs where if you burn a personal day, nobody says what.

I'd never 'picked up' a woman before. Never just met a girl and asked her out. But Lilly was right in front of me, and making sarcastic jokes about how slow the line was moving eventually gave way to actual conversation, about books and comics and bad adaptations, a little *Star Trek, Doctor Who*, our jobs (she's a paralegal), living situations (I had three awful roommates), and on and on.

I have a tendency to overshare.

I was pretty damn charming, although I burned through alotta my best anecdotes. Once you tell somebody about the time you accidentally walked onto the set of *Law & Order* and got yelled at by Jerry Orbach, where do you go?

Anyway, by the time we were in sight of the author, it was almost 4. I figured what the heck. I have a long history of falling for girls in my orbit—classes, dorm, work—but never properly asking them out. Never actually saying the words, 'Do you wanna go on a date?'

I know what I wanna say, but I can't. It's like a force field. Like I'm trapped inside my body, banging on the walls, screaming for somebody to lemme out. But nobody can hear. This was different. With Lilly, on line, I didn't have any of those hang-ups. We'd just met. If she said no, we'd get to the author, get our 90 seconds each, and then we'd never see each other again.

Only good outcomes.

Anyway, she said yes. Which was amazing and terrifying and then I was talking to the author and trying to explain the whole 'I don't know anything about my dad but the comics he left behind' story and making an absolute mess of it. Blurting. Forgetting where I was in the story. I don't think he understood much of what I was saying, but he seemed genuinely pleased to see the original comics.

The last thing he said was, 'Say hi to your dad for me.'

I said, 'See you later!'

That night, when I came home, I slid the comics back into my dad's long box. 'These were your dad's' was all my mom would ever say about them. Had ever said. Will ever have said.

Shit.

I found the box when I was a kid. In the basement, under the stairs, under a pile of dusty old flea market board games, in what we called 'The Harry Potter Closet.' Which was less transphobic at the time. Mom wouldn't talk about Dad, but she lemme keep the comics. Wildly inappropriate for my age, but I don't think she ever read any of them.

Far as I knew, she was never into that stuff.

I devoured them all. Three-hundred and twenty-one comics:

Animal Man #1-26
Camelot 3000 #1-12
Death's Head #1-7, #9-12
Doctor Who #1-23
Doom Patrol #19-64
Maxx #1-14
Sandman #1-67
Shade the Changing Man #1-57
Starman #0-5
Swamp Thing #20-64
Watchmen #1-12

I read those comics over and over growing up. Like they were clues. Like they could tell me who my dad was. Why he left. Like he was *in there* somewhere, and I just had to find him. Bring him back.

People thought Alec Holland came back. That he was the Swamp Thing. But Alec Holland died in a fire. The Swamp Thing was just this plant monster walking around with Alec Holland's memories.

Alec Holland wasn't Swamp Thing. My dad's not those comics. I know that.

But they're what's left.

THREE

That night, the night she died, the police detective asked me if my mom had any enemies. Like she knew anybody. Like anybody knew her.

'Yeah,' I told her. 'No enemies.' No enemies. No friends. And a son who hadn't talked to her in two years. She didn't deserve that.

It shoulda been easy to pick up the phone. Write an email even. I get so distracted. By the littlest things. I go to do the dishes, but a light bulb's out. Go looking for a light bulb, and the junk drawer's a mess. I'm halfway through reorganizing the junk drawer, when Lilly asks me why the dishes aren't done. It's always whatever's in front of me. And if it's not in front of me, it doesn't exist.

It was like my mom didn't exist until she was the burnt-out light bulb.

And now I can't not change the light bulb.

No. Sorry. That doesn't make sense.

I get distracted. Forget things. Sometimes I remember, but it's easier to pretend I didn't. People are hard. It's so much easier to retreat from the world. From expectations. From disappointments.

My childhood was chaos. Was that her fault? Mine?

She was always working two jobs. Three jobs. Barely home. The house was a disaster. I was always making myself sick. What was that? Depression? Anxiety? She'd leave me home by myself to watch cartoons or eat junk food.

When I grew up, moved out, it was just easier not to come back. She sold the house, moved into an apartment, then a smaller apartment, then a smaller one. I had no home to go back to. Just a woman that I didn't know.

That doesn't mean I didn't love her. Didn't wanna know her. I just didn't know how to reach out. But was that my fault? My responsibility? When did she reach out to me?

The closest we ever came to correspondence were the emails she'd forward me. Bad dad jokes from the oldest, jankiest corners of the internet. Knock-knock jokes. Silly stories that ended in puns. Lists of words that sounded funny the more you said them.

'Flabbergasted.'

I don't even know where they came from. Somebody told me that email forwards are what people used to do before there was Facebook. Mom was never on Facebook. I tried once. Sent her a link. That was me trying. A link. She never replied.

I told the detective that she barely went out. Didn't know anybody. But was that true? How would I even know that? Because she never went out when I was a kid? Never brought anybody around? Because every time I visited her as an adult, I felt more and more claustrophobic? Blinds drawn. Shelves crammed. Every flat surface stacked with papers, books, magazines. Dirty dishes left out. Dust everywhere.

She'd always been dead, as far back as I could remember. Of course, she didn't know anybody. The living can't see ghosts. Except.

Except she sent me those emails. Ghosts don't send emails.

One night, couple months after she died, stupid shit like that was rattling around in my head. It was past midnight. Lilly had gone to bed hours earlier. I had a game controller in one hand, coffee in the other. Sometimes the caffeine helps me sleep.

Except, I thought, sometimes she sends me emails.

I set down my controller and my coffee. Pulled out my phone. Tapped and swiped and tapped again. Somebody sent her those emails. I pulled one up. Scrolled down.

Joke-a-Day@y——.com.

Well, okay then.

FW: 52 Poultry Jokes That Will Make People B-Gawk.

And then I saw it. Saw them. It'd been so long, I'd forgotten. Or maybe I'd never noticed? It'd been so long, I forget whether I'd forgotten. But I wasn't the only one she sent those forwards to. There were three other names in the To field. Three other people she was corresponding with. If you could call it that.

Three suspects:

Joan.Simpson@g——.com
EvelynD@schwartzhamm.com
BraddockFanatic@yahoo.com

Simpson was my mom's grandma's maiden name, I think. So a cousin, maybe? I started there. Tried to find her on Facebook, but there are alotta Joan Simpsons out there. Broke down and wrote her an email instead:

Dear Joan,

This is Pat Hinkle, Angie Hinkle's son. I'm sorry to say that she passed recently. I was putting her things in order when I came across your email address. Were you and my mom close? Had you spoken recently? Is there anything you can tell me about her? What was she like as a kid? Also, who are you? How are we related? Did you know my dad? Did you murder my mom? Do you live near us? Within murder distance? Do you know anybody else who'd want her dead? Do you wanna solve her murder with me? Why can't I write an email without going completely off-the-rails? Did my mom go off-the-rails? Is that why you killed her? If there are so many Joan Simpsons on Facebook, how did you manage to get <u>Joan.Simpson@g——.com</u> as your email address? Do you know somebody at G——? Did you kill the original Joan Simpson and take her g—— account? Why do I drink coffee to go to sleep?

Thanks,
Pat

My brain can get away from me sometimes. Mosta the time. I deleted everything but:

Dear Joan,

This is Pat Hinkle, Angie Hinkle's son. I'm sorry to say that

she passed recently. I was putting her things in order when
I came across your email address. Were you and my mother
close? Had you spoken recently?

I knew I was supposed to say something else. Something
grown-up and not insane-sounding. 'Sorry for your loss'? 'Thank
you for your time'?

I stared at the screen. Closed my eyes, took a breath, opened
them.

Same words.

I can always blurt out nonsense. Write these words. But when
I try to edit myself? To choose my words? Choose the right
words? The same thing always happens. Thoughts crash into
thoughts. I lock up.

Trapped behind the force field.

I tried. I did. I started a half-dozen half-sentences and
couldn't finish one of them. Typed, deleted. Typed, deleted. My
chest was tight. Just couldn't.

Ten minutes, twenty minutes, half-an-hour I sat there,
thumbs hovering over the touchscreen keys. Typed. Deleted.
Typed. Deleted.

I wanted to cry. Wanted to throw up. I throw up a lot.

I hit send. Before I could stop myself. It was gone. Out there.

Had you spoken recently?

Then nothing.

Phone slipped from my hand. Into the crack between the seat
cushion and the arm of the couch. I'd fish it out later. Closed my

eyes. Reclined.

The phone fell through the couch. Hit the floor with a clonk.

S'okay. I drop my phone a lot.

I'd get it later.

FOUR

I woke up to a buzzing somewhere.

Got up, scratched the gunk from my eyes. Wasn't sure what time it was. Middle of the night. Spent five or ten minutes looking around the apartment. Whatever had buzzed wasn't buzzing anymore. Tried to be quiet so I wouldn't wake up Lilly. Didn't do a great job. Every floorboard creaked. Every footstep was a stomp.

Walked into a bookcase. It came outta nowhere.

Eventually I remembered my phone under the couch. Fished it out. Joan had replied.

Thank you for reaching out to me, Pat. I'm so sorry for your loss. I only met your mother once, years ago, at our grandmother's funeral. She seemed nice. Sometimes she sent me email forwards. Please extend my condolences to the rest of your family.

Joan

Probably took her 30 seconds to write that. Fuck, I envy her. <u>EvelynD@schwartzmanhamm.com</u> wasn't hard to figure out. Mom worked at Schwartzman-Hamm for a few years. Till the Pandemic. They're accountants. Mom was doing secretarial work for them. Found Evelyn Darden on LinkedIn. Job: Senior Administrative Assistant. Boss secretary.

The next day I opened up an extra tab on my work laptop and wrote her an email:

Dear Evelyn,

This is Pat Hinkle, Angie Hinkle's son. I'm sorry to say that she passed recently. I was putting her things in order when I came across your email address. Were you and my mom close? Had you spoken recently?

No reason to reinvent the wheel. I added:

Please extend my condolences to anyone who might have known her.

Thanks,
Pat

I hit send and closed the tab.
My phone buzzed at lunch. I set down my sandwich.

Dear Pat,

I'm very sorry to hear about your mother. She was a nice lady. I haven't spoken to her since she left, although she sometimes sent me joke emails. I assume that's how you found my email address. I'm so sorry for your loss.

Evelyn Darden
Schwartzman-Hamm Accounting
"Accounting for Everyone"
evelynd@schwartzmanhamm.com

'She seemed nice.' 'She was a nice lady.' These people didn't know her.

That just left BraddockFantatic@yahoo.com.

Couple days later, I got around to googling them. Nothing. Tried 'Braddock Fanatic' too, but that didn't help. Tried Braddock Fanatic without the quotes. Got pages and pages and pages of random results. None of it helpful.

Before, I knew I was talking to a relative. A co-worker. But here I knew nothing. Did this Braddock Fanatic even know my mom?

I wrote an email. Fewer words:

I'm Angie Hinkle's son. Did you know her?

Hit send.
The reply came in under a minute:

Did something happen?

She died. I'm sorry.

Please call me.

In their last email, they left a telephone number. I didn't wanna call. I knew I had to.

Week later, I was on the toilet at Starbucks with the phone in my hand, staring at the numbers I'd typed into it. Daring myself to tap the call button.

For the hundredth time maybe.

And then I did. Startled myself. Dropped the phone on my foot. It bounced and hit the floor. I stood up, startled, peed on the phone a little. By accident. Pulled up my pants. Swore. Picked up the phone and wiped it down with a wad of toilet paper.

And I heard this small voice: 'Jesus, who is this?'

I dropped the toilet paper in the toilet, brought the pee-phone up to my lips. You're grossed out? This was happening to me. And I said, 'Braddock Fanatic?'

There was a pause. I tried to zip with one hand, but it wasn't gonna happen, unlocked the stall, elbowed my way out. There was a guy at one of the urinals giving me stink eye. I gave him stink eye. Now everybody had stink eye.

Stuck the pee-phone between my shoulder and my ear, zipped and buckled. Looked at myself in the mirror. Lunatic.

The voice on the phone snapped me out of it. 'Patrick? Is this Patrick?'

Was it? I looked at the lunatic in the mirror. He looked back at me. Lunaticishly. 'Yeah,' I said. 'Yeah, I'm me. Who's this?'

The guy from the urinal left without washing his hands. I don't blame him.

'Marvin,' said the voice. Said Marvin. 'I'm your mother's friend Marvin.'

Never heard of him. 'I've never heard of you.'

'We…' Another pause.

I thought about whether I should wash my hands while I was still on the call. Or flush. I looked back at the stall.

'We haven't spoken in years,' he said finally. 'You said she died?'

Dribbles of pee. Toilet paper unspooled. Dangling.

'Patrick?'

Also, I'd pooped.

'Pat?'

'Are you local?' I asked. 'Can we meet?'

FIVE

Lilly had to nudge me awake when the call came. The night Mom died. I didn't recognize the number. 'Probly a spam?' I mumbled. She socked me with her pillow. It was two in the morning.

I closed my eyes. Tried to think coherent awake-person thoughts. 'Now would be an excellent time to refinance!' 'Test your carbon monoxide detector today!' That sorta thing. Deep breath, then I swiped up.

I'm not sure who I spoke to. Don't remember much of what was said. They told me my mom was dead. That she'd been killed. That I should come now. I remember repeating the word 'killed' back to them phonetically, like I'd never heard it before. Lilly was already getting dressed. I asked for the address. 'We're in her apartment now,' they said.

I didn't want Lilly to come. She'd never met my mom. Now seemed like the wrong time. I was too asleep to explain. She called an Uber. The driver was chatty. Two stars.

There were two squad cars outside. The detective met me at the door. I don't remember her name. I wanna say Marilyn, but that's somebody I went to college with. I'll call her Marilyn here. She tried to prepare me. Said that word again. 'Killed.'

I followed her in. Convinced Lilly to wait in the hall somehow. Mom was in the living room, face-down in the shag carpet. The blood seeped in. Made a dark halo on the rug around her head. I was there to identify her I think, but the first thing Marilyn wanted to know was if her apartment always looked like this. Boxes were taken down from the shelves, stacked in awkward places. Piles of papers cascaded from flat surfaces down to the floor, between and behind furniture. Looked like maybe mold was growing on a dish in the sink.

I nodded. I hadn't been there in two years. Maybe I shouldn't have nodded.

A man was taking pictures of everything. A woman was dusting for prints. Probably the first time anybody had dusted in there ever. That's not true. I'd dusted once. A man was going through papers from one of the many, many cardboard boxes. 'What's all this?' he asked.

I shrugged. 'Correspondence, probably?' Why did I say that? Correspondence with who? Whom? Whom.

They rolled her body, just for a moment, just part way, just long enough for me to see her face. The rug had left this impression, this weird zig-zag pattern. And I found that as long as I observed that pattern, I didn't hafta see the rest of it. What was done to her.

'Yeah,' I said. 'That's her.'

I asked Marilyn if she knew what happened. If they'd caught somebody. Apparently, a neighbor was coming home late. Saw the open door, the busted lock, called 911. Too late.

I asked about her pants. Her lack of pants. Marilyn thought she was reassuring me when she said, 'Her underwear hasn't been disturbed.' Somebody broke in. Surprised her. She was alone. It was late. Probably she just wasn't wearing pants.

Except. I remembered all the nights when Mom would fall asleep on the couch, wake up, drag herself to bed. Wake up in the morning with her jeans still on.

All the nights. All of them.

Where are your pants, Mom?

SIX

I wasn't sure if this Marvin was a suspect or just a way to connect with my mom. Maybe both? He was local, and he agreed to meet me at a diner on the Lower East. I was a few minutes late. Early for me. Honestly, how can anybody time their arrival down to the minute? On New York trains? As far as I'm concerned, just arriving is a victory.

He wasn't there when I got there. Nobody sitting by themself or waiting awkwardly by the entrance. Unless he brought friends? Unless the host was Marvin?

'Are you Marvin?' I asked the host. She said no.

I considered my options and decided to wait awkwardly by the entrance.

A man arrived a few minutes later, at least my mom's age, balding, overweight, short-sleeved button-down half-tucked, glasses, scruffy, thick moustache, Italian maybe, sweating like he powerwalked the last three blocks. I didn't recognize him.

'Marvin?' I asked as he approached. And he nodded.

'Patrick,' he said. It wasn't a question.

We went inside, got a table. Marvin studied the menu. Ordered a Diet Coke. Dabbed his brow with a napkin. I ordered a coffee.

The first question I asked him was 'How long have you known my mom?'

'Decades,' he told me. Glanced up. He was still flipping through the menu. 'Since before you were born.'

'Then why have I never met you?'

Drinks came. Marvin ordered a BLT, no mayo. I wasn't hungry. I asked again.

'Angie and me got into a fight. A long time ago.' He fiddled with his straw. Swirled his soda. 'We hadn't spoken in years.'

'Hadn't?'

He looked up, just for a second. 'Never will now. Shit. Sorry.'

He drank his Diet Coke. I drank my coffee. I had so many questions, but the force field. I didn't know how to start.

'What do you do?' he asked. A safe question.

I shrugged. 'Office stuff. Except not at the office anymore. They keep threatening to re-open.'

'Yeah. Me too. I miss people sometimes.'

I nodded. It was a lying nod. I think maybe he was lying too.

The waiter brought Marvin his BLT. Marvin pulled the toothpick out of each wedge and tore off a little piece of the lettuce, set it to the side of his plate, and then reassembled them. Set the coleslaw aside. Set the pickle aside. It was a little hypnotic. And somehow familiar.

'What did you fight about?'

Marvin took a bite of his sandwich and thought. '*Regulus*,' he said between chews. 'What else was there?'

I sat up. 'The *Bomberman* character?'

He laughed. A short staccato laugh that seemed to surprise even him. 'You're Angie Hinkle's son, and you don't know what *Regulus* is?'

I tried to remember the Wikipedia page. I answered weakly, 'The… smelting process?'

'Oh, Patrick,' said Marvin. 'You don't know anything, do you?' And he grinned, and he slurped down the last of his Diet Coke. There was a light now in his eyes. I didn't see it before. He was dead when I met him. Like Mom. A ghost. A burnt-out bulb. But now?

'I got a question to ask you,' he said and, God, he was almost giggling. 'Maybe the most important question anybody's ever asked you or ever will. You ready?'

I nodded. Hesitantly.

'Do you own a VCR?'

I don't. Obviously. I told Marvin that, and he straight-up laughed in my face.

He said, 'Kids today!' Probably. This is maybe a good time to mention that I'm writing this all down from memory. I might get the words wrong sometimes.

Also, not sure if I mentioned this already, but I'm bad at remembering stuff.

He pulled out his phone and opened up YouTube. 'There aren't alotta good clips on here,' he explained. 'The rights holder's a dick.' He thumbed through the menu.

'Is this about the… TV show?'

Marvin smirked. Set down the phone on the table. Turned it to face me and tapped the little triangle. The video played. The opening credits to a sci-fi spaceship show. A bad transfer off old media. The music blared. Ship looked cheap. Physical model. Brassy and boxy. Flying through the stars as the actors' names flashed across the screen. Some very British names. Two different Nigels. And then the logo.

I wondered whether I should tell him about Mom's last words. Not yet. 'You were fans,' I said. Sometimes I need to say things out loud to really understand them.

Marvin laughed again. Mom was dead, but suddenly this guy was having a great time. He pocketed his phone. 'Were we fans? Patrick. We were *the* fans! We ran the fucking fan club. Those were the best years of my life!'

I tried to imagine my mom in a fan club. As a fan of anything. As anything except the woman who came and went, worked and slept and occasionally remembered to boil some pasta or dethaw fish sticks.

'She really never told you?'

I looked at this guy. Marvin. This stranger-in-short-sleeves. This liar, maybe. This killer, maybe. He didn't know her. He knew some other woman maybe. Why was I here? Because she'd sent him email forwards? She sent Cousin Jane and Evelyn the Boss-Secretary forwards. None of them knew her. This guy. This guy.

I stood abruptly. Chair scraped. Apologized. Too much. Excused myself. 'I gotta go. Gotta go.'

And I went. Caught the R uptown. Was gonna go home. Lilly was home. I didn't. I couldn't. I missed my stop. Missed many, many stops.

Tried to breathe. Woman in a facemask sat across from me. Asked if I was okay.

'No,' I said, sharper than I meant to. 'You?'

She shook her head. Looked away.

Got off the train at my mom's stop in Forest Hills. Walked the eight blocks to her building. Front door key still worked. Inside, the caution tape was still up. Hadn't heard from the landlords. Must be pissed they don't have the apartment back yet.

Inside key worked too. Ducked under the tape. Closed the door behind me. Smell was heinous. Think maybe they cut the power without clearing out the fridge, but I wasn't about to check.

Half-expected to find Mom's outline taped onto the floor. But maybe they only do that in movies? Instead, there was just the absence of her. Without her there, the bloody halo that she left behind in the shag carpeting looked more like a hole.

I laid down beside it.

I shouldn't be here, I thought. Closed my eyes. Whispered her last words. 'I've been thinking a lot about *Regulus*.' About some thirty-year-old TV show. About some fan club?

'I've been thinking a lot about *Regulus*.' There was something about the way she said it.

'I've been thinking a lot about *Regulus*.' Sing-song.

'I've been thinking a lot about *Regulus*.' No. Not sing-song.

I bolted up.

It's a goddamn lyric.

SEVEN

Lilly planned our second date. We went to an NYU bar that she used to go to when she went to NYU. I think she wanted me to know she went to NYU.

She told me the story of how she shoplifted a dress when she was fourteen. Asked me what the worst thing I ever did was. Probing for my inner bad boy.

I told her about the one time my mom hit me. Really hit me.

I was little. Seven, maybe. Was at home after school by myself. Mom had to work. I heard a noise. A creak, maybe. Convinced myself there was a robber in the house. Went to the safest place I could think of, my mom's room, and hid under the covers. Fell asleep.

The next part I only put together later. Mom came home late. Couldn't find me. Looked everywhere. Panicked. Wandered the neighborhood. Realized she didn't know who to talk to. Didn't know any of the neighbors. Didn't know who any of my friends were. From door to door to door, just falling to pieces. 'Have you seen my son? Do you know my son?' Was too scared to call the cops. Scared they'd lock her up. Take me away. She was a mess when she finally got home. I woke up to just heaving sobs. Crawled out from under the covers to ask her what was wrong. 'What can I do?'

That's when she hauled back and

Lilly wanted to find my inner bad boy. She found her wounded bird.

I moved into her place during the Pandemic. When everything was locked down. When everybody was dying. It was nice to have one person.

The last time I saw my mom alive was 2019.

No, that's wrong. We Zoomed once.

We used to be so close. She took me to see a movie. *Treasure Planet*. I forgot *Treasure Planet*.

I was, what? Seven? That tub of popcorn was bigger than my head. And she lemme drink some of her Coke. We laughed and booed. Somebody tried to shush us and my mom threw popcorn at them! I think it mighta been her birthday? My mom's birthday. Not the person she threw popcorn at. It coulda been both of their birthdays? That woulda been weird.

Her. On that day. That one day. Maybe. Maybe she coulda been a fan of something. Run a fan club. Loved life. Had passion. Met somebody.

Had a kid.

And then? And then everything that came after. Was it me? Was it me then? Did I ruin it for her? Did I ruin her life?

Did I kill her?

EIGHT

I rewatched those damned *Regulus* credits thirty-four times. There were no lyrics. And the tune wasn't the tune Mom sang that night. And Google couldn't find me a song with those words.

But I was certain.

I knew that tune. I wasn't sure how, but I knew it. Had she sung it to me as a child? Why couldn't I remember? I mean, I don't remember lots of things. I forget to turn the burner off once or twice a week. Regularly take two or three times as long in the shower 'cause I forget whether I washed my washed my back or rinsed my hair. Start on one thing, get distracted by the next.

Sometimes I forget what Lilly is saying to me as she's saying it.

But a song? I remember every commercial jingle from my childhood. From back when people watched commercials. I remember every bit of random *Star Trek* trivia I've ever read off Memory Alpha. If I close my eyes, I can remember every comic panel in my dad's comic book collection. When Buddy Baker looks out at the reader in *Animal Man* #19 and says, 'I can see you!' I remember.

Is that a clue? Can Dad see me?

Don't get distracted.

I knew that tune.

Marvin would know. If it was a song? All I had to do was pick up the phone and ask. Or I could text him. I didn't even need to use my out-loud words. But could I trust him? He was literally my only suspect. My mom's secret friend who she wasn't on speaking terms with because of some decades-old fight. He says. Except she sent him email forwards. Was he lying? Is he? Is he lying to me because he killed her? Is he lying to me because he's my dad?

The timing of it. *I can see you.*

A fact about those comics, that collection, is that the very last of them are cover dated March 1995. I was born in December 1995. I figured that out when I was a kid. I guess I was a failed detective back then too. My theory was that Mom had a one-night stand, then stole a guy's comics when she made her escape.

I was a kid. It didn't hafta make sense.

But two friends? They cross the line. Fought about it. Never spoke again? Maybe.

That was two questions for Mister Marvin.

But before I could ask him, I had to know more. Had to speak his language. I had to learn whatever there was to learn about this TV show, same way I studied those comics. Which makes it sound like some titanic undertaking, but really I was just gonna google some more.

Lilly complained when I was scrolling at dinner.

'You ever hear of a TV show called *Regulus*?' I asked.

'British show? From, like, the 70s or 80s?'

'Yeah. You know anything about it?'

Lilly stopped to consider. For all our differences, Lilly's a geek like me. Better adjusted, sure. But she has a head for this stuff. Sometimes, if an argument's coming, I can distract her with some geeky bit of geekery.

'It was one of those post-*Star Wars* shows,' she said, 'like the original *Battlestar*. But British, so cheap. Maybe some people from *Doctor Who* worked on it? Or am I thinking of *Blake's 7*?'

I compared her memory to the Wikipedia page. 'No, that's all right. I mean, maybe that's true of that other show too. How many seasons?'

Lilly closed her eyes and scrunched her nose. Her thinking-scrunch. Hands down her cutest feature. 'Three? No! Four.'

I made the buzzer noise. 'No, sorry, you were right the first time. Although. They were on hiatus for a year between the second and third seasons, so you're kinda right too?'

'So what? Eighty-one to—'

'Eighty-three to eighty-six.'

She nodded along as she cataloged the fact for some future trivia night. 'And what's the premise? I mean, why are they having episodic adventures in space?'

I read straight from the Wikipedia page. Tried to do an announcer voice, but mostly it just sounded like me talking: '"Five criminals awaken from cryo-sleep to find that their prison transport ship is damaged and falling into a star—"'

'Is the star Regulus?'

I grinned and nodded. 'It is. Good work. "Together, they

discover a mysterious second ship in stable orbit and make their escape. At first they believe this new shi—"'

'Is the ship also called Regulus?'

I laughed. 'Stop it. You're too good at this! Yes. "At first they believe that this new ship, the Regulus, has been abandoned. That is, until they find the skeletal remains of the ship's five-person crew. Their own skeletal remains."'

'Wait. What?'

'Hold on.' I scrolled further down. 'Okay, it's a time loop thing. Like, it's their ship and sometime in the future they'll die flying it back in time, so it can be there to save them.'

'Oh. Well, that's interesting. Do they ever explain how that happens?'

Scrolled some more. 'Yeah, no. Looks like the show got cancelled before they got around to it.'

'Typical.' Lilly was still smarting from *Pushing Daisies*' cancellation. She spaced for a half-second. I could tell she was thinking about Lee Pace. Then she snapped back. 'Why are we talking about a random British show from the 80s?'

I froze. I wasn't ready to share my investigation. 'Um,' was what I said. I might have also gulped.

'Um?'

I'm not good at lying. 'A friend from work mentioned it?'

Lilly frowned. 'You don't have friends from work.' Accurate.

I shoved a large pile of spaghetti into my mouth to buy myself time. Held up a finger. Made an incomprehensible noise with my mouth full. She took a sip of wine, but did not break eye contact. I really hate her sometimes.

I made it a solid ninety seconds before propriety demanded

that I swallow. 'I mean I hate everybody and one of the people I work with, who I hate, mentioned it, and I was curious, but I remembered that you don't like it when I say I hate everybody because of how it reflects on you, and so I was trying to do the thing you suggest where I pretend to like some people, so I don't seem weird.'

'And?' she asked.

'And?' I repeated back to her.

'And how do you think that's going right now? On a scale of one to ten.'

'A… very normal five?'

I didn't ask Lilly any other questions about *Regulus*.

NINE

If you can break into a crime scene once, why not two or three or twelve times? I kept expecting somebody to catch me, but no one ever did. Until they did.

Until then, I had my run of the place. The small, cluttered, smelly place.

One of the police officers had mentioned 'correspondence.' No. I had mentioned correspondence. He'd agreed. Or at least he didn't argue with me. So correspondence or something plausibly correspondency. The first time I came back, the first time after the first time, I came back to find her plausible correspondence.

I helped my mom with most of her moves. Never questioned what I was moving. Remembered moving the same filing boxes from home to home to home. 'Mom, do you need all these?' I might have asked once. She probably glared. I definitely didn't ask twice.

She had a Top Five glare.

Marvin was telling the truth. Or at least part of it. The first box I opened included ten copies of something called *The Yates Pages*. Hand-typed, photocopied, and stapled together. 'The Official Newsletter of the American Fans of Roland Yates.' Dated February 1989. A compilation of artwork, fan fic, convention anecdotes, and news stories. A half-dozen contributors, and my mom and Marvin Casiano as Co-Editors-in-Chief.

Roland Yates was the star of *Regulus*. He played Reginald Braddock, the charismatic rebel scientist who turns a ragtag band of thieves and killers into freedom fighters against the tyrannical Grand Dominion. According to Wikipedia and IMDB, *Regulus* was his one big dramatic role. Before *Regulus*, he was a comedian and TV presenter. In '89, he was filming a show in New Zealand called *Wonder Grumpus* in which, if I've read my sources correctly, he played a talking hedgehog.

The Yates Pages were mostly about *Regulus*, but with a surprising amount of *Wonder Grumpus* thrown in. This first issue I read included some *Regulus*/*Wonder Grumpus* crossover fanfic that was... surprisingly wholesome. And a section called 'The Cricket Corner' with Yates' latest scores from, I dunno, amateur games? On the second page, they printed a letter he sent to the club, thanking them for some Christmas gift they'd sent him: 'Thank you for everything you do and everything you are!'

Reminded me of how those women talked about my mom. 'She seemed nice.' 'She was a nice lady.' Yates didn't know these people.

The rest of the box was press clippings, drawings of the cast of *Regulus* and I guess *Wonder Grumpus*, hand-written notes, and some honest-to-God correspondence. Originals and photocopies. In no discernible order. There were letters to and from Marvin, planning out upcoming issues. I guess he lived in Ohio for a while. Letters from other members of the club, full of suggestions and fan theories. Letters from Yates' publicist in London, which were actually extremely enthusiastic and encouraging. 'Let me know, and I'm sure I can get you another batch of signed autographs!'

This was one box. Of dozens. On the shelves. In the closets. Stacked up in her bedroom. Over the next few visits, I emptied them all and reordered them. One complete set of *The Yates Pages* in chronological order. Then the copies in chronological order. Then the correspondence in chronological order, when there was a date. Then the undated correspondence. Everything else, notes, drawings, whatever, I tried to keep in the original order, although there didn't seem to be any logic to it. I found photocopies of the same cartoon of Yates playing cricket in four boxes.

He's thinking, 'If they think that googly is wicked, they should meet my ex.'

On one copy, there's a post-it with my mom's handwriting on it. It says, 'IS THIS HILARIOUS?'

Is it, Mom?

By the final box, I'd found forty issues of *The Yates Pages* spanning August 1988 to March 1995. Bi-monthly. For seven years. Shit, Mom. I've never done anything for seven years. The last issue recounts a trip that Mom and Marvin took to London to see Yates in *Cinderella*. He played the Fairy Godmother, and they make a point of explaining that 'It's not weird because it's a panto.'

I dunno what that sentence means.

There was a picture of Mom and Marvin and Yates-in-drag in front of Cinderella's coach. I don't think I've ever seen a picture of Mom that young. Or that that that joyful. I did the math. She was just a few years older than I am now, but she's just

And Marvin! If this picture was anything to go by, Marvin is super, super, super gay. Huge smile. That moustache! Buff. Spikey hair. Hot pink tank top with a picture of Yates' face on it.

So maybe not my dad?

Yates looked ridiculous, but I'm sure he was supposed to look ridiculous. And preening. Look at my adoring fans! Look at my vassals!

And that was it. The last issue, at least that I could find. March 1995. A month late. Then nothing. March 1995. Fuck, fucking, fuckity March 1995. *The Yates Pages* ended abruptly. Dad's comic collection ended abruptly. And some motherfucker fucked my mom.

I took a moment, in her smelly, little apartment, surrounded by seven years of her life measured out in stacks, to wonder:

Did any of this mean anything? Would any of this get me any closer to the truth? To who killed her? Whom? No, definitely who.

Anyway, the next time I went back to the apartment they arrested me.

TEN

Okay, it's not that I hate everybody. That's just a thing I tell Lilly, because it's easier and less embarrassing than the truth. I like most people mostly. Envy them. But also they are sooo exhausting. Paying attention to them is hard. Knowing how to react to every different thing they say? Being friendly when you see them? Stopping to smile and greet them and say their names? So many people have names. It's too much.

Sure, one day you might think, 'Okay, I'm having a good day. Why don't I say hi to the security guard?' And that's fine. But then what? The next day they expect it. Doesn't matter if you're in a good mood or a bad mood. You gotta remember. Stop. Focus. And then what if they wanna have a conversation? Fuck that shit.

Or say you go to the same bodega every day for coffee. Suddenly, the bodega man starts calling you 'Sugar Man,' because you want four sugars in your coffee. You don't wanna be Sugar

Man. Co-workers talk about their gardens. Your roommate smokes a bowl in your living room. Lilly compares this year's gas bill to last's.

I dunno, Lilly! They're different years. We're coming out of a Pandemic for God's sake.

All of it. Superheroes put on masks to pretend they're somebody they aren't. That's what I do. Pay attention. Nod your head. Polite smile. Pretend to pay attention. What did he say? Just agree. Comb your hair. Not like that. Tell a joke. Eye contact. Polite smile. Polite wave. Nod. Nod.

I don't hate people. I envy them. *I hate them.*

I used to have friends. It's easier not to. When I was a kid, I cheated. I played *Dungeons & Dragons*. Bunch of us would get together at the library after school. Roll some dice. Eat some snacks. Do funny voices. You didn't hafta talk about anything real. You didn't even hafta be nice. 'Are you offended that my half-orc thief insulted you? Well, sorry. He has a Charisma of 6. There's nothing I can do.'

I wish I had a higher Charisma.

Did we bond? Sorta. Did I ever set foot in any one of their houses? No.

Did I actually like *Dungeons & Dragons*? I dunno. Did Mom actually like this *Regulus* show? This Roland Yates guy? I dunno. What does it mean to like something? To love something? Or someone? Does it matter who or what it is? Or is it just a thing to feel a thing about.

'I've been thinking a lot about *Regulus*,' she sang.

Yeah. Me too, Mom.

ELEVEN

'I'm gonna need you to raise your hands above your head, sir,' is the first thing the cop told me. Then he told me to stand up.

'Sir,' he repeated.

I swear, I tried.

'Sir.'

I really did.

'Sir.'

I apologized. 'I gotta use my hands!'

That's the closest I ever came to death, I think. So far. That cop did not find my piss-poor flexibility either funny or charming. Thankfully, eventually, I made myself clear. I remain unshot. Pushed myself up, raised my hands above my head again, and stepped out of my paper Stonehenge. 'Am I... *not* supposed to be here?' I asked in my most innocent voice.

I swear, if it was just the one cop there without his partner, I think I'd be dead right now.

Instead, they cuffed me and read me my rights and drove me down to the station.

They put me in an actual interrogation room. That was the best part. With the table and big mirror and the overhead light. I actually said, 'You know this is the best part, right?' I turned to the mirror. 'Right?'

Detective Marilyn came in with her partner. Young guy, real babyface. I don't remember his name either, so I'm gonna call him Other Marilyn. I was hoping for a Good Cop/Bad Cop dynamic, but they were both just sorta Medium Cops?

'You understand your mother's apartment is still an active crime scene, yeah?' said one of them. Probably. Unless one of the cops said that in the car over? Somebody definitely pointed that out. At some point. I remember stipulating that. I said, 'I stipulate that.'

It was definitely Marilyn who asked me what I was doing there. I said cleaning, because it seemed like a bad idea to tell the detectives that you're trying to out-detective them. Okay to out-clean them probably.

'Cleaning?' she said back to me. Incredulous.

I shrugged. I was manifestly bad at cleaning. I oozed it. 'More… straightening, I guess?'

'Well, you can't do that!' said Other Marilyn. Emphatic. He actually hit the table with the side of his fist. He was really going for it. I dug it. I think he wanted to be Bad Cop.

'It's a crime,' Marilyn added. Matter-of-factly. Not Good Cop or Bad Cop. Just Clarification Cop.

I apologized. Can you get out of crimes by apologizing? I said I was just so sad that my mom was dead, and her papers were all

I have left of her. They seemed to buy that. Marilyn said, 'Look, Pat. You seem like a nice guy.' She doesn't know me. 'But if you're in there moving things around, it can disrupt our investigation.'

I was pretty sure nobody but me had been in that apartment for weeks. Months, maybe. 'What investigation?' I asked. 'What are you investigating?'

Marilyn looked at Other Marilyn. Other Marilyn looked at Marilyn. Marilyn shrugged.

'The thing is *is*,' said Other Marilyn, 'nine times out of te—'

'Ten times out of ten,' Marilyn corrected.

'Nine times out of ten,' said Other Marilyn, 'case like this? It's just a random B and E. Somebody's hopped up on drugs. Looking for cash. Things go wrong. But there are some people—'

'Not us,' Marilyn clarified. See? Clarification Cop.

Other Marilyn glanced over to the mirror. 'Other cops. From other places.'

'There's a serial killer,' said Marilyn. 'Out west. Similar MO. Blunt-force trauma. Nothing sexu—'

'It's the pants, mostly. He takes their pants.'

'Probably a coincidence.'

'But these things,' Other Marilyn complained, 'they can get political.'

'What's important,' stressed Marilyn, 'is that you let us do our jobs. Let us sort it out.'

'A serial killer?' I asked. It sounded like nonsense. Made-up. 'Out west? Like… Hoboken?'

Other Marilyn shook his head. 'They're calling him the—'

Marilyn cut him off. 'Do not tell him the name. It's an awful name.'

'It's literally the only good part of all this!'

I told them now I had to hear the name.

Marilyn closed her eyes. Rubbed her forehead. 'The Pants Bandit. They're calling him the Van Nuys Pants Bandit.'

'Van Nuys, California?' I asked.

'It'd be an outlier, for sure.'

I just stared for a while. Kinda made a face, I think. Eventually I started laughing. 'You think that a serial killer from California, who steals people's pants, flew all the way across the country, took a train out to Flushing or whatever, killed one woman, stole her pants, and then flew back to California to keep killing people and stealing their pants?'

'Not us,' Marilyn clarified. 'Other people think that.'

'And if it's not the—?'

'Nine times out of ten,' said Other Marilyn.

And then they uncuffed me. Told me to stop going to my mom's apartment. That I'd get her stuff back eventually. Once this pants guy got caught.

I rubbed my wrists. Not because they hurt, but just because I'd seen people do it on TV. Started to leave. Stopped. Apologized. 'Can I ask you one more thing?'

And I swear I wasn't doing a Columbo. It's just, in that moment I saw my mom's face. Before. After. And the bloodstain that looked like a hole. Like a hole in the universe.

And what was at the bottom? Was there a bottom?

I had a hunch. I dunno where it came from. Maybe it climbed up outta that hole.

Nobody stopped me, so I asked them. 'The injury, was it consistent with a… cricket bat?'

I'd caught them off-guard. Flabbergasted. Other Marilyn said something unintelligible. Marilyn didn't say anything.

But she nodded. Slowly, maybe unconsciously. She nodded.

TWELVE

Mom owned a cricket bat. I never asked about it. She kept it down in the Harry Potter Closet with Dad's comics. I always assumed it was for paddlings. That, if I asked about it, I'd get the paddle. It went with her from apartment to apartment. Even as an adult, it gave me this feeling of dread. The implied threat. Just to pick it up. Just to touch it.

'I can still whoop you.'

But looking back, it was just a cricket bat, wasn't it? The threat was all in my head. As if my mom even cared enough to hit me anymore. But why a cricket bat? Did she own it because Roland Yates liked cricket?

The cops were very interested in my hunch. The Pants Bandit used a hammer. Or mallet. My mom's face wasn't hammered. Wasn't… malleted?

They asked if my mom owned a cricket bat.

They didn't know. Which means they hadn't found it. Which

means

'Years ago,' I said. 'We used to watch cricket together as a kid. On TV. ESPN-something. We had tacos. It was great. But she sold all her cricket stuff a couple moves ago.' None of that's true. I'm not sure why I said the thing about tacos. Mom hated tacos. She thought they only came with guacamole, and she thought avocados were a scam. Sometimes me talking is me just desperately putting one word after another until the sentence ends. It hardly ever ends well, but here I'd just told this amazingly, uncharacteristically convincing lie, so I did the smart thing, and I abruptly turned and left.

Were they suspicious? I dunno. They didn't stop me.

I checked my phone as I walked out. Of course, Lilly wanted to know where I'd been. She'd left me many, many texts. Wanted me to meet her at some karaoke bar on the Lower West. It was already getting late. Who lives like this? Whatever. If I did her thing and she had a good time, she maybe wouldn't ask about where I'd been or what I'd been doing or whether I'd been arrested or if I had any theories about the Van Nuys Pants Bandit.

My one lie was already pushing it.

I arrived a little past eleven. It was a piano bar. Boo. That meant no stage, which was nice, but also the piano guy had to know your song and you had to know the words and probably nine-out-of-ten songs sung were gonna be show tunes. It was crowded. Everybody was singing 'Part of Your World.' Ugh. Fuck Disney. I squeezed in next to Lilly by the bar. Said hi. Quick kiss. Ordered a beer.

'Who are we here with?' I asked. She told me. I couldn't hear her over all the thingamabobs and whatzits. She pointed, unhelpfully, into the crowd. I thought I recognized Jane, maybe? I have trouble telling people apart sometimes.

At one point, Lilly sang 'Bad Reputation.' The whole crowd was with her. She pulled me up to the piano after. I swigged the last of my beer and accepted my fate. Handed it off to her.

'What can I play for you?' asked the piano man.

I sputtered. No excuse. I'd been there for an hour. I coulda thought of a song. I just said the first thing that came to mind.

'Uh. Piano Man?'

'Yes?'

"Piano Man."

He frowned and turned to his keys. I'd committed some kinda karaoke piano bar *faux paus* maybe. But he started to play. However reluctantly. And I sang.

'It's nine o'clock on a Saturday…'

Oh fuck. I faltered. Maybe it was compassion, but the whole bar took over for me. Everybody. Lilly. Jane-maybe. Everybody just belting it, but me.

I was still stuck on the first line.

'It's nine o'clock…'

I knew that tune.

'It's nine o'clock…'

I've been thinking a lot.

'It's nine o'clock on a Saturday…'

What. The. Actual. Fuck.

'I've been thinking a lot about *Regulus*.'

THIRTEEN

I didn't wanna call Marvin. I knew I had to call Marvin. I didn't wanna call Marvin. I knew I had to call Marvin.

I couldn't go back to her apartment again. Not after the cops. And I'd read everything there was to read about *Regulus* on the World Wide Web. I had to know why my mom's last words were sung to the tune of Billy Joel's 'Piano Man.' Had to know what it meant. Was there more to the song? Was it a message? Like my dad's comics? Like… Marvin's comics? Gay Marvin's comics?

Gay people can have kids. Is that what happened?

I didn't wanna call Marvin. I didn't wanna imagine my mom having sex with Marvin.

I knew I had to call Marvin.

Lilly could tell I was more agitated than usual. Which is to say, usually I'm agitated. This was more. Day after day, and I was getting worse. Panicked. Distracted. Listless. I called out of work one day. I never call out of work. I mean, work is a laptop on my couch. Why bother?

Lilly found me one evening, half-asleep. On the couch. My head kinda hanging off and one foot up over the back. *Voyager* was streaming from the Roku. Paris and Janeway were lizards again. Lilly whacked me with the mail, which was usually my signal to sit up like a normal and maybe look at bills with her. I sat up. Scooted over. She tossed the bills on the coffee table. She didn't wanna talk about bills.

Uh oh.

'Hey,' she said. And she smiled. She put a hand on my shoulder. What was happening? 'Do you remember that show *Regulus* we were talking about a while back?'

I squinted at her. Counted to ten in my head. Slowly answered, 'Yeahhh?'

'Apparently, they still do little conventions. There's one coming up at the end of the month at this hotel out on Long Island. I thought maybe we could go as a laugh?'

I nodded, slowly at first, then faster. Kissed her. Pushed her back against the arm of the couch. Reached a hand under her shirt. We hadn't done it in a while. She was down.

The convention was three days long. Our tickets were for Saturday. It was at a hotel in Ronkonkoma, which was fun to say at least. Honestly, I hate going to Long Island almost as much as I hate going to Staten Island. I hate going to all the New York islands.

Ryker's Island? Probably also bad!

We took the LIRR. The RR to LI. Hate. Hate. The New York subway system I can follow. There are numbers and letters and colors. The LIRR just explodes my brain. I let Lilly buy the tickets and just do what she says. Sometimes that's the best, easiest option.

The con was called 'Hyperspace 34.' As in, they'd somehow already done thirty-three of these things. For a show that hadn't aired since the 80s, that wasn't on streaming or Blu-ray or even DVD? That you couldn't even pirate? Yeah, I tried that. All Marvin had been able to show me was a YouTube of a VHS that wasn't even a minute long. But these people were still showing up, year-after-year-after-year.

We took an Uber from the train station. It was a two-minute drive, but who wants to get lost in Ronkonkoma? There were no turns. Probably it woulda been fine.

I've been to New York Comic-Con. Just mobs of people spilling out of the Javitz Center in their costumes and geek tees. This was not that. Walking up, the only sign that something outta the ordinary was happening was a little person sitting on a bench by the entrance in a white wig and blue face paint smoking a cigarette.

We avoided eye contact.

There was a sign in the lobby, a whiteboard that said 'Welcome HYPERSPACE 34!' in flooshy letters with a few hastily drawn stars. So at least there was that. Lilly and I asked at the front desk. We were dressed all regular. Lilly thought it'd enhance the ironic distance. The guy said, 'Are you sure?' Like maybe we were asking by accident. I said, 'Yeah, no, we have tickets.' And I held up the email we'd printed out.

He pointed down the hall. Said to follow the signs.

The signs were just pieces of paper taped to the walls with arrows, which was fine and also made me wonder why people spend so much money on signs. At the end of the hall, they had a professionally-printed banner that read:

HYPERSPACE CON
CELEBRATING THE GREATEST TELEVISION SHOW EVER

No year, and the blues were starting to look a little faded. I didn't hafta be a detective.

Beneath the banner, a woman sat at a folding table with a stapled printout, a cash box, and a roll of red raffle tickets. I found out her name later, but I won't mention it yet. She had frizzy gray hair and thick glasses and a white t-shirt with a cartoon of Yates-as-Braddock drawn on it in magic marker. Yates was doing Munch's *The Scream* and saying, 'I thought YOU were flying!'

Impenetrable.

Lilly smiled politely, because she's good at that, and gave the woman our names.

'Hinkle?' she asked. Surprised. Oh no.

'Yes,' said Lilly. 'Patrick Hinkle.'

This was a bad idea. I said, 'One second.' And I maneuvered Lilly to the side. Arm around the shoulder. 'Do you need to go to the bathroom?' I asked her. 'We should really go to the bathroom.' We were right by the bathrooms. It was the perfect plan.

Lilly frowned. 'I'm sure they have bathrooms. I'm sure we can come out and use these bathrooms.'

'But what if we're having so much fun!' I said.

Lilly's frown frowned. I can't explain it any better.

'We are here to have fun, aren't we?'

The actual words I was using weren't important. I was just stalling until Lilly's inner-prudence kicked in. It was like Lilly's Prime Directive: Always pee first.

'Fine,' she said. 'Fine, fine.' And she turned and walked into the ladies'.

No time to waste. I went back to the table and started saying words. 'Yes, I'm Pat Hinkle. Angie Hinkle's son. And this is my first convention, first *Regulus* convention, and my girlfriend doesn't know about any of this, and I don't wanna freak her out. She's very, um, normal. And. So if you could ixnay on the Momnay, I would very much appreciate the thing that would then be happening after that with my girlfriend and the not knowing about the things, could you?'

And this woman smiled at me, the biggest, broadest, most generous smile I think anybody has ever smiled at me. Her teeth were… not great. But otherwise, Top Five smile. 'Oh, of course, honey. I'm just so happy to see you.'

And I smiled back. Honestly, my teeth aren't much better. I thanked her. Made a mental note to find her later. She checked off our names from her list and signed the back of two raffle tickets and gave them to me. I held them up to show Lilly as she came outta the bathroom.

'All set!' I said. 'Let's go in.'

FOURTEEN

My first time on Long Island, I was I-dunno years old. It was a Saturday. Mom was supposed to be at work, but instead she woke me up early-early and got me on the train. She had the cricket bat with her, so I didn't argue or ask questions.

Later on, I figured out that she'd been fired from her weekend job. She was always getting fired from one job or another. There were always more jobs. But that day her, me, and the cricket bat went to Long Island. It was still dark when we got there.

We walked from the train station to the parking lot of a Dunkin' Donuts. She told me to hold back. Hold the cricket bat. Maybe that's why she brought it. So I could fight off goons?

What year was this? How old was I? I remember I wasn't old enough to walk through a dark parking lot unless I was holding Mom's hand.

And then she met somebody under the lights.

He was, I dunno. A man, probably. Blurry, maybe? No, that sounds wrong.

I don't think I could hear what they said to each other. Wouldn't remember if I did. But they were arguing. For-real arguing. With spittle and finger stabbing and now and then she'd point at me, and they'd get louder.

I didn't think about it then, but I wondered later if he was my secret dad. Did he look like me? Do I look like him? Am I blurry? Half-blurry? Blurry on my dad's side?

Anyway, it didn't go well. He threw up his arms. Stalked off. She stormed past me. Said, 'We're going.' Those words I remember.

And I said, 'Aw, can't we at least get a donut before we go?'

And she whipped around, and she glared and she scowled at me and she said: 'We. Can't. Afford. Donuts.'

And then we walked back to the train. As the sun rose over Long Island. I fell asleep on the ride home. Sank into her arms. Slept deep. Safe in knowing that if anybody messed with me or her, they'd get the paddle. Dreamed that this was every day. Me and her on weird, secret adventures to all the New York islands.

When I woke up, I was home. She was gone. Off to some new job.

I saw her again, now and then.

I see my dad in dreams sometimes. And in those dreams, I know him. He's a part of my life. Mostly we walk the old neighborhood, and we talk. Like Jack Knight talks to his dead brother in *Starman* #5. Except his face is a blur. His voice, an echo. I ask him for advice, and he changes the subject. Asks me how work is. How Lilly is. Says he'll hafta go soon.

I tell him to wait till Mom's back, but he shakes his head. His blurry, blurry head.

In *Starman #5*, Jack meets his brother in a graveyard. It plays out like a dream, but they say it's not. His brother's dead, but they say it's not the afterlife either. It's not this, it's not that. The whole comic, they never say what it actually is, this thing that's happening. How they're together. A mystery without an answer. In *Starman #5* at least. Cover-dated March 1995. It's maybe the last comic in my dad's collection. If he'd stuck around, I'm sure they woulda explained it eventually. Explained the thing, beyond death, beyond dreams, that connects us to the people we've left behind.

Or to those who left us.

FIFTEEN

The entire convention was just four rooms:

Seller's Room
Screening Room
Autograph Room
Panel Room

That's not including the hallway that ran between them, which seemed to be the preferred place for folks to stand awkwardly in my way and catch up. Also, there were vending machines. I got myself a Pepsi. Everybody was older than us, no surprise. My mom's age on up. And I mean *up*-up.

Some solid cosplay. Two Reginald Braddocks. Three man-in-all-black-I-didn't-know-yets. One person dressed up as the ship. With lights! Lilly made a point of going over and telling them how much she liked their costume. No official *Regulus* merch, so alotta folks came in their old con shirts. Hyperspace 27 was apparently a good shirt year. Other folks made their own custom shirts. At one of those websites maybe or by-hand like Ticket Lady.

One woman wore a black tee with white letters that read:

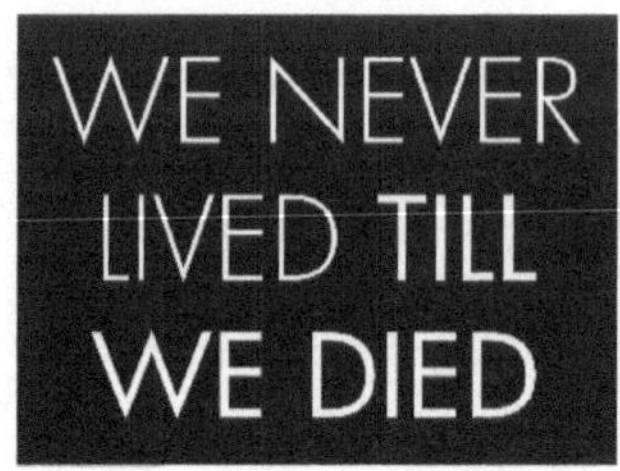

Which is weird, right?

'What should we do first?' asked Lilly.

There were printed schedules taped up beside some of the rooms. I took notes on my phone:

Screening Room
2 PM – 'Screams of the Bargrons'
3 PM – 'If Wishes Were Fishes'
4 PM – 'Small Arms'
5 PM – 'Guns at Dawn'
6 PM – 'Time Loop'
7 PM – 'Time Loop'

Autograph Room
3 PM – 'THE' Becky Stratton
5 PM – Alfie Norton

Panel Room

2 PM – Our Favorite Episodes
4 PM – Miggsy's Meanderings
6 PM – The Future of *Regulus*?
8 PM – Talent Show

It took a while to type all that. Probably coulda taken a picture? By the time I was done, Lilly was gone. Maybe she'd told me she was going somewhere. I looked around. Tried to guess what Lilly might have decided to do midway through me typing things into my phone.

Buy things? Buy things. I walked into the Seller's Room. It was small, especially in comparison to the bigger cons I've been to, but also in comparison to smaller ones. A local comic shop had set up in one corner. Mark's Comics. They had alotta *Star Wars* and *Doctor Who* on display. No *Regulus*, obviously. There were a couple artists doing sketches, *Regulus* with some other stuff mixed in. I thought about asking for a *Wonder Grumpus*, but didn't. And there was a couple crocheting together at one table. I thought maybe they'd just sat down to knit, but when I walked up, I saw the business cards for their Etsy shop. They were knitting *Regulus*-themed hats. Because of course they were.

Lilly was talking to the woman from the comic shop. Only Black face in a sea of White. And even younger than us. Felt bad for her. Lotta shops set up tables at cons to offload their backstock. But a con this small? She was bound to be losing money.

As I walked up, Lilly said something, and they both laughed. Is Lilly funny? I put my hand on her shoulder.

'Did you finish writing everything down?' she asked.

I explained that I did and showed her the list. She smiled with so little effort. I wanted to check out at least one or two episodes, just to be sure this was all real and not some elaborate prank, but then I thought the panels might be informative, and I at least wanted to talk to 'THE' Becky Stratton. She was one of the main cast members. But she played Miggsy, the telepathic alien pilot, so probably she'd be at the 'Miggsy's Meanderings' panel too.

Alfie Norton, I did not know.

Halfway through explaining all this to Lilly, she asked me to stop and pick one thing to do 'right now.' It was almost two o'clock, so I said 'Bargrons.' Then 'Screening Room,' because the word 'Bargrons' by itself has no content.

So we did that. Lilly wished the comic shop woman good luck, and we walked over to the screening room, which was small and dark, with a single TV up front on a rolly cart. And a VCR. We came in a couple of minutes into the episode. Some nerds shushed us. We're also nerds. I'm not judging.

In the episode, Reginald Braddock and his second-in-command Nil were stranded on a swamp planet and something-something-radiation-something was slowly mutating them into low-budget plant zombies. Nil was the man-in-black that people were cosplaying. Played by one of the two Nigels. Braddock was an idealist, but Nil mostly just wanted to do crimes. Do crimes and, in this episode especially, not be a plant zombie.

Nil figured out a way off the planet, but to do it he had to leave Braddock behind. Which he did, gleefully, until he realized that Braddock had the fuel they needed, so Nil had to go back for him.

The production values were cheap as shit, but the actors sold it. I can see how people coulda gotten into it. Yates as Braddock was undeniably charming. Nigel-Number-One as Nil was so hilariously loathsome it was brilliant. And right at the end, we got two minutes of 'THE' Becky Stratton as Miggsy the Telepathic Alien Pilot doing schtick, and *of course* she was the little person in blue face paint I saw chain-smoking outside.

People were walking out before the episode ended, which seemed weird until I realized they'd all probably seen these episodes a billion times already and also because the autograph line was forming for 'THE' Becky Stratton. Lilly insisted we stay through the end credits, 'because people work hard to make these things,' which put us all the way at the end of the line.

Of course, Lilly and I have been in long lines before. It's where I do my best work.

Alotta times I have trouble talking to other people. Saying the things I most wanna say. That force field I wrote about. But the stakes here were so impossibly low. I leaned forward and asked the couple ahead of us, 'Enjoying the con?'

One of them turned and gave the briefest nod. Lilly smiled at me. Social skills are one of her turn-ons.

'PATRICK!'

I turned. The Ticket Lady had joined us at the end of the line. 'Enjoying the con?' she asked.

I nodded. Lilly maybe laughed. She said, 'We just watched "Scream of the Bagrons." Do you like that one?'

Ticket Lady said she did. Especially the part where Nigel took his shirt off. And then she fanned herself with one hand. Might have actually said the words 'Hubba-Hubba.' Added, 'But it's no "Desolation Factor," amirite?' When she didn't get an immediate reaction from either of us, she clarified: 'Yates. Butt.' They both laughed.

Then Lilly asked how long she'd been involved with the con. My favorite part of what was happening was that I didn't need to say or do anything. Ticket Lady said this was her twenty-somethingth as an organizer, thirty-somethingth as an attendee. 'They used to be bigger,' she said. 'Those first few were magical.'

Then she looked at me. I forced a grin. Oh no. Be cool, Ticket Lady. 'What about you, Patrick? Is this what you expected?'

I looked around. Standing in a line? Honestly, I thought the lines would be shorter. 'Was Becky Stratton a big get?' I asked eventually. 'Do you get somebody from the main cast every year?'

'They all used to come: Roland. Nigel. Other Nigel. Lenni. Now it's just Becky every few years when her stand-up schedule lines up.'

She seemed bummed, so I offered, 'But you have Alfred-Somebody!'

'Alfie's an easy get, Patrick.' There was an edge to her voice that caught me off-guard. 'He wrote the genie episode.'

I guess she doesn't like 'the genie episode.'

I considered whether I could ask Ticket Lady, then and there in front of Lilly, about the lyric. I didn't see how. Or ask her about Marvin. *The Yates Pages*. Or cricket bats? Mom was dead. Is dead. What was I even doing there? To watch Reginald Braddock turn into a dollar-store Swamp Thing? To get an autograph? To spend $3.75 on a can of Pepsi?

'Are you staying for the talent show?' she asked. 'That part's always my favorite.'

I looked at Lilly. She looked at me with a smile on her lips and a NO in her eyes. 'Maaaybe,' I said.

When we finally got to the front of the line, I paid 'THE' Becky Stratton $25 for a signed headshot. She wrote 'To Patrick and Lilly! You make me feel old!' I had time for one question. I panicked. Asked, 'Do you like cricket?' She did not. Maybe rolled her eyes? 'Roland was the cricketer. He played professionally for a few years before he started acting.'

Was? Was Roland Yates dead? Did it say that on his Wikipedia page? And I missed it? Or forgot? I forget alotta things. 'Is he dead?' I asked.

'THE' Becky Stratton took my hand, looked into my eyes, and said, 'I'm so sorry, luv. This may come as a bit of a shock. But Roland died a couple decades ago.' And then she laughed. Hard. Cry-laughed. Banged the table. Tried to apologize but broke into a giggle fit.

Ticket Lady stepped around me, asked Stratton if she needed a glass of water. Between giggles, she answered, 'I needed… water… twenty-five years ago.'

I waited with Lilly till her Uber came. It was fun, she said, but she'd gotten the experience. I told her I was gonna stick around, maybe watch another episode or two, then come home. I think we were both lying.

Somewhere else, 'THE' Becky Stratton was still laughing.

SIXTEEN

By the time I met Lilly's dad, he was deep MAGA. Thanksgiving 2018. The midterms hadn't gone well for him. He was not pleasant to be around. Lilly told me he used to be less whatever he was now. I wasn't sure. He was a small-town banker. Upstate New York. I think he maybe was the plot to *It's a Wonderful Life*. Like, the unwonderful parts. He seemed petty. Thin-skinned. Somehow deeply paranoid and ridiculously gullible at the same time.

Also, he left his wife when she got cancer. In case you were looking for any redeeming characteristics. I mean, fuck him. You may not remember this, but Thanksgiving weekend 2018 was a billion and seven days long. It was awful.

We stayed at his house. The house he bought when he walked out on Lilly's mom. She's fine, by the way. Lilly alternated holidays back then. The guest room he put us in used to be Lilly's, but you couldn't tell. He primered the walls. Hung one of those 'Footsteps in the Sand' things up. Y'know, the one that goes:

'LORD, how come when things got really rough, there was only one set of footprints?'

'Because you had cancer, jackass. People with cancer are gross.'

Or, I forget. However that goes. What I'm saying is, I didn't like the guy. But Lilly wanted him to like me. She told me to call him 'sir' and not to talk politics. Which I did for a while, because those are easy enough rules to follow till they're not.

'For a while' wound up being seventy-two hours, give or take. Long enough for him to tell me every unfiltered racist xenophobic misogynistic homophobic transphobic anti-Semitic or Islamophobic ableist ageist bullshit thought that passed through his bigoty-bigot bigot-brain.

And did I contradict him? I did not. Because I'm a coward, mostly. Mostly, I tried to say 'oh' or 'hmm' after anything he said. One time I said 'that's an interesting perspective!' It was not. I might have said 'uh huh' once or twice by accident. But I didn't call him a sniveling little shit *at all* until late Sunday afternoon when, out on the porch, over lemonades and apropos of absolutely nothing, he turned to me and asked, 'Ya think the reason she had a miscarriage was all that drinking?'

After all that, we left a day early. Day one billion and six. I told Lilly it was because I had to email a file to Japan from my work laptop. I'm sure the truth got back to her eventually.

He died last year. The Ivermectin didn't help. Ten days he didn't go to the hospital, and by then it was too late. They wouldn't let us in to see him. They had to have the funeral outside.

It was not well attended.

Afterwards, back at the house, she pulled a beaten-up, dog-eared copy of *The Moon is a Harsh Mistress* off a bookshelf. Flipped through it. Her dad had lent it to her when she was eleven. Her first Heinlein. She'd underlined half the book.

She didn't say, but I think he hit her.

We got drunk and fucked in his bed.

I asked her why.

'Because it's a much more comfortable bed.'

I meant why did she keep coming back. 'After everything he said and did and was. Even now,' I said. 'We don't need to be here.'

I might be paraphrasing.

She thought about it for a while before she answered. Looked out the window. Out towards the lake. 'Because he was nice to me once or twice. And I don't like giving up.'

I really, really like giving up. It's good for my soul. Sometimes I can't. I dunno. I just get stuck. I didn't. I can't.

I should have told her.

SEVENTEEN

Ticket Lady found me after 'Guns at Dawn' and asked if I wanted to get dinner with the girls. The girls were her, 'THE' Becky Stratton, and the woman from the comic shop, who I guess maybe owns the comic shop? And maybe sponsored the con?

I didn't want to, because people, but I said yes, because I have a murder to solve.

We went to the Red Lobster down the street. 'THE' Becky Stratton apologized on the walk over. Ticket Lady had told her who I was. Becky knew my mom. Knew how crazy Mom was about Yates. I told them Mom had just died, and that seemed to hit them both really hard.

Comic shop woman didn't have much to say. She just observed.

I didn't tell them how Mom died. But I told them I didn't grow up with *Regulus*. Didn't even know about the show till recently. They weren't surprised. Mom had dropped out of the fandom so many years ago, but none of this woulda existed without her and Marvin.

Comic shop woman got us a table, bought a round of drinks.

I had so many questions, but also only one question: 'Can you tell me about the song?'

Ticket Lady smiled. 'The Anthem?'

'The Billy Joel thing,' I clarified.

They fucking started singing it:

I've been thinking a lot about Regulus,
How we nearly fell into the star…

They clinked mugs. Laughed. I grabbed my chest. Couldn't breathe quite right. Comic shop woman pushed me a glass of water. Ticket Lady offered me an 'awww.'

I drank.

'It's a filk,' said Ticket Lady. I didn't know what that meant. 'In fandom, we do parody songs. Well, not parodies. Songs to the tune of other songs. They're called filks. I'm not sure why.'

'And this one…? You called it "The Anthem?"'

'THE' Becky Stratton explained, 'The show went off the air in '86. By the time it started airing in the States, we were already done. But you Yanks were all so passionate, your mum, Marvin Casiano, Lydia here. You tried so hard to save the show! We all came to that first con. Roland went to the talent show. He sang your mum's song.'

'We all sang the song,' said Ticket Lady. Said Lydia. That's when I found out her name's Lydia. 'You know, for a long time after that, your mom said that was the best day of her whole life.'

'Till she gave up on fandom?'

'Until you were born, Patrick.'

When I was little, I had a nightlight. And when you wound it up, it'd play a tune. 'Twinkle Twinkle Little Star.' And every night, Mom would sing me to sleep to that song. Over and over, till the nightlight wound down. And if I wasn't asleep, she'd stop anyway. Wherever the nightlight stopped. Sometimes mid-word. And she'd shrug. And she'd say, 'Sorry, Patty. That's all you get.'

Sometimes, I'd ask her to wind it up again. Plead with her. 'Sorry, Patty.' She never would. When did I stop asking?

'Am I the reason?' I asked the girls.

'Reason for what?' asked Lydia.

'Did she give up *Regulus* for me?' I told them I knew I was born around the time *The Yates Pages* folded. Told them I knew Mom and Marvin had a fight, maybe after they got back from London.

'Oh honey,' said Lydia. She put a hand on my shoulder. Looked like maybe she was gonna start crying. Was I already crying? 'Your mom? Marvin? They fought all the time. But she didn't leave fandom after you were born. After *The Yates Pages*. The two of them did *The Nil Set* for two, three years after that.'

'Okay,' I said. And then I closed my eyes. Took a long, deep breath. Opened my eyes again. 'What the fuck is *The Nil Set*?'

EIGHTEEN

The Hyperspace 34 Talent Show began with fifteen minutes of 'THE' Becky Stratton stand-up. No *Regulus*. Nothing about the con. Probably the same routine she does everywhere: Her kids. Her exes. Covid jokes. No little people jokes. Oh, and she was out of make-up. She was out of make-up at Red Lobster too. Sorry, I shoulda mentioned that.

And the crowd wasn't very engaged. There were still people filtering in, finding their seats. A few chuckles. A few side conversations wrapping up. It's funny how they treat her. Like an old friend who's also their God who's also sometimes invisible.

I couldn't tell from her expression. She's a pro. But did it upset her? Did it matter to her? That these people were so obsessed with something she did forty years ago, but didn't seem to give a damn about her actual career. I dunno. She put up with it. Wore the make-up mosta the day. Signed autographs. Posed for pictures. I wonder how much they pay her.

And then the turn. A transition so smooth I almost missed it. From traffic jams on the New Jersey Turnpike to Braddock and Nil and Miggs on the *Regulus* flight deck, pursued by Zoon Raiders. And how the camera man kept falling asleep while they were taping. And the crowd came alive. They applauded. Roared with laughter! I saw a few people mouthing along, word-for-word, like a favorite song. They all knew this story. And the next one. And the next.

And by the time she wrapped up, they were on their feet. The whole crowd. Whooping and hollering. I was on my feet! Good grief, why was *I* on my feet? And she was beaming. Because she wasn't just another aging road comic. Not here. Not tonight. Tonight, she was 'THE' Becky Stratton.

And then she introduced the costume contest. No surprise, the spaceship won. Apparently, the spaceship wins every year. The person in the spaceship costume. They do other costumes. Last year, I'm told they did 'Braddock-as-a-horse from the genie episode.' And because they always win, apparently the real winner was the person who came in second? Somebody's grandma in a Nil costume. She cried and gave a short speech. She thanked 'this crew, this family, these friends' and everybody applauded.

It was just good energy. And it carried on through the talent portion of the talent show. Lydia introduced the acts. There were dancers. Two jugglers! A magician. One guy did a beautiful acoustic version of the theme on his guitar. A couple of people tried their hand at *Regulus*-themed stand-up. It did not go well. People cheered anyway. And, of course, there were singers. 'Filk' singers, I guess? More songs about *Regulus* to the tune of songs you know. And Lydia was right. They absolutely were not parodies. They were sincere. Achingly sincere. Or, when there was a joke, it was sung with a smile and a wink. With an understanding that they would never make fun of this show. This shared experience.

Then Lydia called Comic Shop Woman up to the stage. This is when I found out her name. Sasha-something. Lydia thanked her for supporting the con, and Sasha said it's what her dad woulda wanted. More applause. Some sniffles, I think. Tears.

Who was her dad? Nevermind. I dunno who my own dad is. I can't be worrying who other people's parents are.

After that the lights dimmed, and Sasha sang a slow sad song called 'Braddock and Nil Met as Strangers.' She sang it a cappella and her voice was just okay, but the lyrics were surprisingly heartfelt for somebody I'd originally assumed was just there to sell comics.

And though they sometimes fail,
When they're resolved,
They'll tread the path till they're absolved.

Heartfelt, but also a few people were laughing, which seemed weird/rude? Later, somebody explained that she wrote her song to the tune of an old Disney cartoon. *Chip 'n Dale: Rescue Rangers.* Fuck Disney. Anyway, big round of applause, especially from the folks who got the joke, then Lydia asked everybody to stand. They were gonna close out the talent show the same way they do every year:

With the Anthem.

There was some kinda commotion at the back. I was up front. With everybody standing, I couldn't see. Some swearing and shoving. Marvin? I worked my way to the aisle. I saw Lydia heading around the other way.

It was him. By the doors. A couple of the volunteers trying to hold him back. He was brown-bagging a 40. Looked very drunk. Dirty and scraggily and sweaty. His t-shirt half-untucked. A Hyperspace 27. 'Not without me!' he was shouting. 'You motherfuckers don't sing shit without Marv!'

Lydia approached timidly, hands out in front of her. 'Hi Marv,' she said. 'Why don't we talk in the hall? I'll buy you some M&Ms.'

Marvin struggled with the two volunteers. They were all in their 50s or 60s. It was sad. 'I don't like M&Ms anymore,' he grunted. 'M&Ms shouldn't be blue.'

I got in close to them and put my hand on one of the volunteers' shoulders. 'I got this,' I said. Why did I say that? Did I got-this? Probably not. But I somehow confidenced my way into one volunteer then the other standing down. And then Marvin had nobody left to fight with, so he stopped fighting. Looked at me. Slumped his shoulders, bewildered.

'Patrick?'

I took him by the arm and walked him out into the hallway. They shut the doors behind us. 'I can pick out the blue ones,' I told him. He nodded slowly. I bought a pack from the vending machine. 'Did they used to not have blue ones?'

'They let people vote in 1995. It was awful.'

I started picking out the non-blue M&Ms from the bag, handed him a handful. 'What're you doing, Marvin?'

He was sorta swaying. Shrugged. 'I wasn't gonna come till I was gonna come, y'know? I haven't missed a Hyperspace in years.' Ate an M&M. Two.

'Is this about my mom?' I asked him.

'Why didn't you tell me?' he whined. And he just shoved the whole fistful in his mouth. He was crying and munching and sweating and stinking and it was just ridiculous. Sad. Pathetic. Ridiculous.

'I did tell you,' I reminded him. 'That's how we met.'

'I mean that...' He swallowed. More M&Ms than anybody should swallow all at once. 'That somebody killed her?'

I didn't have an answer. I mean, I did have an answer. My answer was, 'Because I've only got one suspect, and he is you.' Which didn't feel like a thing I could say. What could I say? I had to say something. I was just standing there. Time was passing. Tick tick tick.

Marvin held out his hand. His palm open.

'I...'

He gestured with his fingers. Gimme.

'I...'

'More M&Ms.'

I picked out another handful of not-blue M&Ms for him. 'It just didn't come up,' I muttered.

'I get that,' he said, before he shoved the next handful into his mouth.

I patted him on the back. 'We should go inside. They're gonna do the thing.'

He nodded, and we walked back in together.

NINETEEN

They waited. When we walked back in, they were all waiting. The fans gathered around us. The volunteers who were ready to throw down five minutes earlier were offering Marvin hugs now that the fight was out of him. Lydia too. 'THE' Becky Stratton called him a wanker 'but our wanker,' and the crowd laughed and cheered.

They dragged Marvin up to the stage. Somehow, I got carried along. And Lydia was up there. And Sasha. And Spaceship and Second-Place and Volunteers 1 and 2. And how did I suddenly know all these people? And then the music kicked in. An instrumental track.

Billy Joel on piano.

And they sang:

I've been thinking a lot about Regulus,
How we nearly fell into the star,
When the ship's AI brain went a little insane,

And took things a little too far!

We escaped to a ship from the future,
Our skeletons at the controls!
It was clear we were trapped in a time loop!
It was clear we were trapped in a time loop!

The next part I knew, so I sang along:

La da diddy-daaa
La da, diddy-da, da-da da da da

Bring me along into hyperspace!
Bring me along for the ride!
'Cause we all wanna have an adventure,
And we never lived till we died!

In our last life, we were all criminals!
In this life, we fight the good fight!
We've fought Bargrons and Zoons and Dominion Goons
And one genie we won't dwell on tonight!

People really hate that genie. Poor Alfie Norton. Whoever he was. Wherever he was.

The music swelled:

I know someday we'll come back to Regulus!
We already know how it ends!
Just one season more, or possibly four,
For this crew, this family, these friends!

Everybody:

La da diddy-daaa
La da, diddy-da, da-da da da da

Oh, bring me along into hyperspace!
Bring me along for the ride!
'Cause we all wanna have an adventure,
And we never lived till we died!

As the song ended, the room erupted into cheers. There were hugs and high-fives and tears. Marvin apologized to Lydia. I think I saw 'THE' Becky Stratton disappear out the side door. Lydia hugged me and whispered in my ear, 'Your mother is always here with us.'

And maybe she was.

The next song played, another instrumental track, up-tempo and jazzy. I didn't recognize it. Whatever comes after 'Piano Man,' I guess.

And we all danced.

TWENTY

'What the fuck is *The Nil Set*?'

Sorry. I forgot about this part. This happened at the Red Lobster. This was important too.

'It was the other newsletter,' Lydia explained. 'The one they did after *The Yates Pages*. About Nigel Kent, who played Nil. It only ran a couple of years.'

I'd been through my mom's papers. There was no *Nil Set*. 'When?' I asked.

Lydia thought about it. 'Your mom's last Hyperspace con was number ten. That was 1998. You woulda been... three, probably? So—'

'Waitwaitwait. Mom brought me to Hyperspace?'

She looked surprised. 'I thought you knew. This is your fourth, I think.'

How could I not remember? Do I not remember things that happened to me when I was three? How far back do normal people remember normally? I tried to visualize my mom pushing me around the con in a stroller, me screaming my baby head off and oh no. No no. Did she dress me up?

'Did she dress me up?'

Lydia cackled. 'First year, she painted you blue! Took her a week to get the gunk off. She never tried that again!' 'THE' Becky Stratton laughed too. Had we met before? All these people. Did they *all* know me?

This was… What was this? It was too much to process. Needed something to hold onto. Facts. Facts are good. 'So *Nil Set* ran from, what, '96 to '98?'

Lydia nodded.

'And she dropped out of fandom after *Nil Set* folded?'

'Yes, but…' Lydia paused. 'Oh, Patrick.' And the joy just drained from her. Her posture. Her eyes. Even the screaming cartoon on her shirt seemed a little sadder. 'It wasn't about the newsletters. It wasn't about *Nil Set*. Roland Yates died in 1998. She loved that man. It broke our hearts. All of us. But I think hers most of all.' She wiped away a tear. 'She walked away after that. We never spoke again.'

She wiped her nose and her eyes with a napkin.

Gross, Lydia.

I reached over. Put my hand on hers. And I said, 'You can use my napkin, if you need to.'

TWENTY-ONE

After that, I don't remember a whole lot. There was drinking somewhere. Lotta drinking. And then a diner. At one point, it was just me and Marvin in a booth with too many pancakes between us and tiny, tiny OJs.

Were there other people with us? Somebody else in the booth? Maybe they'd gone to the bathroom? I remember feeling like I didn't have alotta time, like someone was gone but coming back and I had two questions for Marvin and I could only ask one of them. Because of the time, yes, but also because each question precluded the other:

Did you kill my mom?

Are you my dad?

I had to pick. You can't ask someone if they're a killer, then immediately ask if they're your dad. Or the other way. Even drunk, I knew that.

Did you kill my mom?

Are you my dad?

Marvin was saying something about the speed that TV shows play at in the US versus the UK. Like, time is faster here, so UK shows play slower? Or did in the 80s? Something-something-frame-rate-something. He wasn't leaving many spaces for me to talk. So I had to blurt.

Did you kill my mom?

Are you my dad?

Two yes-or-no questions. That's four combinations of answers. Yes-yes. Yes-no. No-yes. No-no. A two-by-two grid. I could see it, floating in the air between us:

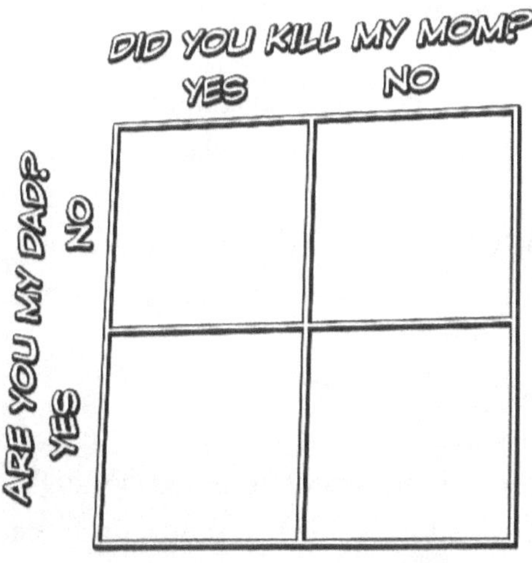

Or at least that's how I remember it.
Did I do drugs? I don't think I did drugs.
Probably I'm just crazy.

All I knew for sure was that the answer couldn't be yes-yes. I don't think I could handle it if my dad killed my mom, right? But if Marvin killed my mom and he wasn't my dad? I dunno. I think I could live with that. Somebody's gotta be the killer. And if it means that this guy I just met who-definitely-isn't-my-dad-in-this-specific-scenario was the guy? Yeah. Yeah, okay.

And if he wasn't the killer? Did I actually want Marvin to be my dad? This guy who, okay, if somebody had to kill my mom, I just decided I was fine with it. Don't I want my dad to be somebody who I wouldn't wanna have killed my mom? Like, if yes-killer and no-dad is fine, then yes-dad and no-killer can't be fine, can it?

Did you kill my mom?

Are you my dad?

Yes-killer and no-dad or no-killer and no-dad good. No-killer and yes-dad or yes-killer and yes-dad bad. That was it then. Decided. The floating grid didn't lie. I didn't want Marvin to be my dad. And, Christ, now he was talking about VHS speeds. Blurt blurt blurt. Just ask him if he killed your mom. Ask ask

    ask

      ask

'Are you my dad?'

Marvin stopped mid-word. Squinted at me. Picked up a tiny, tiny OJ and downed it. While still squinting at me.

Weirdo.

And then somebody came back to the table. I think. Possibly I passed out in my pancakes.

When I was walking home from the train, it was light out. I had thrown up all down my pants leg. At some point. I stopped into the corner bodega for a coffee. The guy at the counter smiled when I walked in. 'Heyyy, Sugar Man!'

Everything hurt. Nothing was worth this. Got to my apartment building. Was Marvin my dad? Why were our OJs so small? Who was there with us? When did I throw up? Is four sugars too many sugars? Inside. Up the stairs. Who were these people? Would I ever see them again? Should I write a filk? Key in the door. Which way does it go? Lilly. Wondered if she was still asleep. 'Lilly,' I mumbled, and the door opened. Lilly was on the couch, cross-legged. Awake. Still awake? Waiting for me. Livid in the living room. Something in her hand. What was in her hand? Small. Black. Oh no.

Oh no no no.

She twanged the strap against the cover.

'What in the actual fuck, Pat?'

TWENTY-TWO

I'd meant to buy something for my stomach. Pepto or Pepcid or probably just a Pepsi? Caffeine calms my nerves. My mom was dead. Holy shit I had nerves.

This was the night she died.

I hadn't been to this CVS before, but I'd passed it. And anyway every drug store I've ever been to is basically the same store. Just rearranged to confuse me. Where was I going? Aisle to aisle, and all I could see was the thatched zig-zag pattern the rug left on her face. And the red. I walked into a display of cheap toy cars. It landed with a crash. Startled me outta my head. Little Corvettes and British double-decker buses and taxi cabs everywhere.

Nobody came. Nobody cared, I guess. I set the display back up myself. Picked up the cars, one by one. One of the side mirrors on one of the taxi cabs had broken off. I put that one at the back. I put all the cars of each type together. I don't think they were like that before, but it felt better to sort them.

It's funny. For somebody as disorganized as me. As bad at basic chores. At taking care of myself. This? It felt good. Calming. Manageable. Satisfying. That I could see a problem and solve it. When nobody else even cared. Who was my mom to those police officers? Nobody. A taxi with a broken side mirror. And somewhere out there, the person responsible. Who knocked over the display? I was alone. The only one who cared.

It had to be me. I would find them.

My brain was on fire. *Is* on fire. Too many thoughts. Need to stay focused. *Needed* to stay focused. Organized.

I seriously considered the Unicat journal. Was it from some cartoon I hadn't seen? It had sparkles.

No, I told myself. Focus. Plain. Boring. Black.

I picked one up. The right one. With the pebbled cover and the strap. I twanged it. Saw the zig-zag. Twanged. Gone. What was I doing? I dunno. What was anybody else doing? Nothing. Maybe I was the only one who existed. Just like there was only this one drug store. The only person in the only place. Except.

Except somebody killed my mom. I wasn't alone.

I thought about stealing a double-decker bus. Nobody would know. I could just shove it in my pocket and walk out. I put it back on the display, on the second shelf with the other buses.

Wait. Shit. Was Lilly with me? She'd come with me to the crime scene. Did she go with me to the CVS? I can't remember. Maybe she'd gone home. Or maybe she was in some other aisle. Maybe she helped me pick up the cars.

'It's okay, baby,' she said. Not then.

This is too much. Too much to remember. I shoulda started writing sooner.

TWENTY-THREE

'It's a journal,' I said. 'I've started journaling.'

I smiled normally. Good job, me.

Lilly didn't look convinced though. Did she think I was lying? I wasn't lying. This is definitely a journal. I bought it in the journal aisle, remember? And anything you write in a journal is automatically journaling. That's just how words work. Whether you're writing about your day or copying out interesting recipes that you find online or sketching out little nature scenes or maybe it's just the words 'I WILL FIND YOU' in big block letters and a list of clues. All journaling.

It was only those last two things.

But Lilly was big mad. Had she read my journal? Should I have been big mad at her? 'Did you read my journal?' I asked her. Big madly.

She was still sitting on the couch. Sorta half-dropped half-flung the journal down on the couch next to her. It landed with an unsatisfying thwuff. 'You mean the journal that's been sitting on the ironing board for the last five months?' Oh. Oops. 'Yes. Yes, I read your… your…' She paused. Considered her words. Possibly rejected a few options. Looked confused. Let out a frustrated yargh. Picked up the journal again and held it out towards me. 'Whatthefuckisthis?'

This. This. This is why I never told her. I didn't wanna be judged. Didn't wanna hafta explain something I have no words for. I made a vow that night. All those months ago. And have I followed through on that vow? I dunno. Sorta. I made a list. Sent some emails. Had lunch. Broke into a crime scene. Sang karaoke. Went to a sci-fi convention. Threw up on my pants.

That must count for something. Yes. I said it. 'I'm gonna find my mom's killer.'

She threw the journal at me. I flinched, and it hit my shoulder. Fell to the floor. She shouted at me. 'You do not have the temperament to solve a murder!'

I bent down self-consciously and picked up the journal. I was crying now. Just a little, I think. I cry more than I probably should. Life is a lot sometimes. 'You've never believed in me,' I muttered.

'Believed in you?' Lilly was standing now. Maybe she was standing before. Pointed a finger at me. 'You're not the Tooth Fairy, Patrick.'

'I mean the other kinda believing!'

She knew what I meant. 'Believing in someone is not the same as believing that they should do stupid shit. Believing in someone means believing that they'll *stop* doing stupid shit *eventually.*'

I pulled the journal close to my chest. 'This isn't stupid shit, Lil. It's… It's my mom's life. It's…' My voice got heavy. Hard to speak. Squeezed my eyes shut. And in the dark behind my eyes, I saw the zig-zag pattern and the color red. The blurry man that might be my dad. The black hole in my mom's carpet, and the hunch climbing out of it. A Stonehenge of papers. Buddy Baker staring at me out of the pages of *Animal Man* #19 and saying, 'I can *see* you!' A baby in blue face paint in a stroller. Throwing popcorn at *Treasure Planet* and disappearing under the covers. Grainy VHS transfers. A two-by-two grid and somebody missing from the table. A train ride home from Long Island. No. *Two* train rides. The nightlight and my mom saying 'That's all you get.'

'It's all I have left of her.'

It was a little while before I opened my eyes again. She said, 'It's okay, baby,' and she said, 'I know,' and she put her hand on my shoulder. And when I finally did open my eyes again, she was holding out her best pen to me.

The one that writes upside down.

'So take it seriously.'

WHAT
WAS

TWENTY-FOUR

I capped the pen. Lilly's pen. Flipped back through the pages of my journal. I'd written twenty-three fucking chapters.

Why chapters? 'So take it seriously,' she'd said. Are chapters serious?

It was dark again. Where was Lilly? 'Lilly!' I called out.

Stood up. Leg asleep. Leg asleep. Pins and needles. Hopped. Shook it out.

'Lilly?'

Maybe she'd left? Couldn't remember. At one point, she'd ordered pizza. There was a plate of crusts next to where I was sitting on the couch.

Lilly doesn't leave crusts. Those were my crusts.

'Lilly!'

I limped into the bedroom. She wasn't there. What day was it? I'd been writing for a while, but not that long, right? Checked my phone. Still Sunday night. Okay okay.

Messages. Marvin. Not now. Delete. Lilly. Play.

Do your thing. Call out sick if you need to. I'll be at Jane's.

Huh. Delete.

Walked back out to the living room. Dropped the phone on the couch. Thwupp. Laid down. Passed out. Dreamt of *Regulus*.

I was on the prison ship, from the pilot episode, the one that fell into the star. Except it wasn't. Wasn't a star. It was a black hole. And not a cool CGI black hole with, I dunno, weird lights and debris getting sucked in. It was just a big flat black nothing in space.

An emptiness between the stars.

And the cast was there. Not their characters. Roland Yates and Nigel Kent and 'THE' Becky Stratton. And some of the other actors, but they were all Muppets for some reason. And my mom was there with them. Not a Muppet. And they were all smiling and clapping each other on the back, and they were singing her song.

I've been thinking a lot about Regulus.

I took my mom by the arms, tried to shake her out of it. 'Mom,' I said. 'We gotta go. We're gonna fall into the black hole!'

And she looked at me, this look of just absolute revulsion on her face, and behind us they were still singing that damned song. *It was clear we were trapped in a time loop.* And she looked at me, this look of just absolute revulsion on her face, and she snarled, 'We. Can't. Afford. Donuts.'

And I can't. Couldn't. I turned, ran for the airlock. *And we never lived till we died!* Pulled a lever. The door opened, and I was whipped out into the silence of space. Into the black hole. Into the emptiness. Stretched, stretched to ribbon. To nothingness. To silence.

There were no more songs. No more of the endless clatter in my head. No doubts. No fears. I simply was. Or wasn't?

No. No, I smiled. I could feel my face again. Feel myself. I was alive and floating across a dark and endless sea. And I was singing to myself. The theme to *Chip 'n Dale: Rescue Rangers*. Because I'd googled it earlier, and it's damned catchy. Fuck Disney.

And for a moment, just a moment, staring up into a starry sky from the endless sea of Regulus, I knew who killed my mom. And why.

Or, I dunno. I thought I knew. One time I had a dream I'd figured out a really great recipe for meatloaf, and when I woke up it was just 'use alotta eggplant.'

When I woke up from this dream, the sun was rising or maybe setting through the blinds.

I sat up. Scratched the gunk from my eyes. Picked my nose, unless you think that's gross. You think that's gross. I didn't pick my nose.

And I considered, seriously considered, whether an eggplant killed my mom.

TWENTY-FIVE

An eggplant didn't kill my mom. I was pretty sure.

I think there was more to my dream, but I can't remember now. Writing down something that just happened seems like it should be easier than writing down something that happened months ago, but dreams are hard to hold onto.

I re-read chapter twenty-four. Am I good at writing? That doesn't seem right.

I needed a plan. Need a plan. Shit. Tenses! See, now I'm in my head, and I've ruined it. Twenty-three chapters in one go, and now it's just nonsense from here on out. Kibble. Knish. Flabbergasted. Focus.

Somebody killed my mom. With her cricket bat. Took the cricket bat and her pants. Forced entry. Coulda been nobody. A stranger. Or the Van Nuys Pants Bandit. Broke in. Mom went for the bat. There was a struggle. The killer took the bat. Beat her to death with it. Left with the murder weapon. And her pants because why? Because they had his blood on them? Or I guess it coulda been a woman. In which case, *her* blood I guess. If. Can a woman kick a door in?

I'll google it later. Anyway. Is that it? No mystery? Just a random B and E on a Tuesday night. That's what the detectives said. Nine times out of ten, ten times out of ten. Shit. Are they right? Sorry, whoever winds up reading this. This is probably a huge letdown.

This whole chapter's shit. Maybe I'll add s'more later.

The sun was setting, by the way. I'd slept through Monday, and after all that and then deciding my mom was killed by some random rando, I couldn't get back to sleep. When is Lilly coming back? Is she ever coming back? Did we break up?

No. She bought pizza and left a message on my voicemail telling me where she's at. When people break up with you, they don't tell you where they're going or buy you pizza.

Maybe they buy you pizza.

I think I need there to be more to this. For my mom's death to mean something. It needs to not be random. I think it needs to be connected to this TV show, to that song, and whatever happened in the late 90s, after Yates' death, that drove her away from the community.

Something else.

Otherwise, what am I? Just a weird guy who's a mess all the time and has all these weird hang-ups and doesn't have a dad?

I'm useless without structure.

I'm not gonna write anything else in this journal unless something important happens.

Sorry.

Whoever you are.

TWENTY-SIX

Something important happened.

Lilly came home on Wednesday. That's not the important thing. I'll get to that.

Lilly came home on Wednesday and asked how it went. I said fine, and she asked if she could read what I'd written. I said, 'Definitely no,' and I could tell she was disappointed.

Shit. I'm letting you read this, and I don't even know who you are. Are you Lilly?

Forget that stuff I said before. Lilly is great.

Besides the fact that she likes most of the same nerd shit I do and does good people-skill stuff sometimes and has a Top Five nose-scrunch and highlights my *Star Trek* books, which I say I don't like, but actually it makes them easier to read. Besides all that, and actually her singing voice is pretty good. Besides all that, she doesn't give up on people. Even when she should, I think.

On her dad. On me. On the New York Mets.

Fuck the Mets.

I think maybe Jane is going through some shit too. Not her mom dying, but shit. I should ask.

Anyway, if you're Lilly.

You're probably not Lilly.

Lilly busted out an awesome fact Wednesday night. This is also not the important thing. 'Did you know,' she asked me, 'that Regulus is actually four stars?'

I did not know that, and also that sounded wrong, so I googled it, and it is not wrong! Turns out Regulus is actually a quadruple star system. Two pairs of stars, orbiting each other. They only figured that out in the mid-2000s, waaay after the show ended.

'Sometimes you think it's just one thing,' Lilly told me, 'and it turns out to be a whole bunch of different, more complicated things.'

'Like a…' I could tell that suddenly we were having a deep conversation, and if I said something deep, maybe we could have sex. 'Like a…?' I struggled for an example of something I could compare it to. 'Like a metaphor?'

She sighed. Corrected me. 'Like a simile.'

We had sex anyway.

I probably didn't need to mention that. We didn't have sex. Or, like, just the normal amount. Shit. I'm in my head again. Important thing!

The important thing was a phone call. On Friday. From Lydia, who I didn't think had my number. 'I didn't think you had my number!' I said. Instead of 'Hello.' I immediately realized my mistake, so before she could say anything, I also said, 'Also, hello.'

She told me Marvin gave her my number. Which makes sense. I'd deleted a few of his messages. I was waiting for an Uber. I asked Lydia, 'Is Marvin my dad?'

'Oh,' she said. Like she knew the answer, but didn't wanna say. 'You should ask him.'

'I did.'

'And?'

'I don't remember. I maybe passed out in my pancakes.'

'Is that a metaphor?'

I told her it wasn't and then remembered that she'd called me about something and then asked her to tell me what the thing was that she'd called to ask me about.

'I was wondering about the cricket bat,' she said.

I'd never mentioned the cricket bat to her. Or anybody. Except the police. Was she the police? I didn't ask her. She probably wouldn't say if she was, and also she definitely wasn't. Isn't. I just said, 'How do you know about the cricket bat?' Normally.

'We all know about the cricket bat, honey. It belonged to Roland. It could be worth a lot to a collector. We just didn't want you to throw it out not knowing.'

Worth a lot to… Shit. Maybe the cricket bat wasn't just the murder weapon. Maybe it was the

'Wait. We?'

'The royal we.'

'What?'

'I always refer to myself in first person plural. I mean, "we do." I mean, "we mean, we do." We mean, "we mean, we mean, we do." I think. We think. Shit. I'm not gonna start that again. Marv. Marv asked. Marv remembered the cricket bat, but said you weren't returning his calls. Maybe you two should talk about it?'

I said, 'Yeah, definitely,' which, why is that the least-committal thing a person can say?

Anyway, I was gonna end the call, gonna hang up, but then I remembered that I'm a secret detective, so I asked Lydia, 'Lydia, if someone was gonna sell the cricket bat, who would they sell it to?'

'A c—'

'A collector, I know. But who?'

Lydia was quiet for a minute. Not a minute. But long enough that I was like, 'Are you still there?'

Lydia's answer came slow and deliberate. 'I just don't... I don't think you should sell something like that, Patrick. It... it meant so much to Ang. We've gotta hold onto the things that matter.'

Which, yeah, that was sweet. Definitely Lydia didn't kill my mom. And I dunno. Maybe I would keep the fucking bat. If I had it. Which I do not. And if I'm gonna figure out what happened to it, who killed my mom and took it, I need to know who'd buy the fucking thing.

So I said, and look I know I know I know, but I said, 'Honestly, Lydia. I just want the money.'

I think maybe I broke her heart a little bit. I heard a sniffle on the other end of the line. Two sniffles. The second louder than the first.

'You do what you want, Pat. I'd start with Sasha Jacks.'

TWENTY-SEVEN

I coulda asked Lydia for Sasha's number, but I couldn't. I mumbled something, and I hung up. I felt like shit. Feel like shit. Shit. I gotta do something nice for her. *She* should have Mom's cricket bat. If I ever find it. If I ever find

I knew one other person who might have Sasha's number. 'Shit.' I called Marvin. It went straight to voice mail. Kidding, no, he picked up on the first ring. Because of course he did.

'Patrick?'

'You asked about the cricket bat?'

'I wanted to make sure you were okay. You passed out in your pancakes.'

That's that confirmed. Brilliant. 'Yeah. Look. Lydia told me about the bat. Said collectors might wanna buy it. Said I should talk to Sasha. Do you have her num—?'

'We should talk.'

'Do you have her number, Marvin?'

'I'm not your dad, Patrick.'

I couldn't

'We should talk.'

I hung up. Stared at my phone for maybe five minutes. Finally texted.

ok

We met up at that same diner. The first one. Not the pancake-splat one on Long Island. The one on the Lower East Side. He was early this time. Ordered the same thing. I got a coffee. All the sugar. I brought comics.

Tried to form a sentence. 'So you're saying that you didn't… um…'

Marvin shook his head. 'I'm a gold star.' I dunno what that means. Do they give out stars for not sleeping with my mom?

'I thought—'

'Angie and I weren't even talking when you were, uh…' He did a gesture. A 'when you were being conceived' gesture. It was weird and awful in its specificity. I waved my hands to get him to stop.

'Gross, Marvin.'

I'd gone over and over the timeline on my way to the diner. Typed it out on my phone:

January 1995 – Mom and Marvin go to London
March 1995 – Dad's last comic (*Starman* #5)
March 1995 – Last *Yates Pages*
March 1995 – Somebody boned my mom

March 1995 – Results of Blue M&M thing announced

Probably the last thing isn't important.

'You musta still been talking,' I insisted. 'It was March 1995. You were still doing *The Yates Pages* with my mom in March.'

'No.' Marvin did this kinda sad laugh-cough-shrug. 'That issue was supposed to be out in February. It was the only *Yates Pages* that ever went out late. Late, because we weren't talking.'

Okay, okay. I dunno why I was trying to prove something that I didn't wanna be true. Maybe, couldn't be true. Do I want a dad that badly? Anway, I had one more card to play.

Well, one more comic. Comics. Two more comics.

'You didn't talk to my mom in March '95?'

'On the phone maybe? Once or twice? To talk shipping.'

Good, good, I thought. Catch him in the lie.

'Okay, so what about these?' I pulled two of the comics from my backpack. Tossed them on the table. *Starman #5*. *Sandman #67*. *Starman* may have landed on a pickle. They were bagged and boarded. It was fine.

And Marvin. The smile on his face. In his eyes? Like he was a kid again. Or, I dunno, like a less old adult. He picked up the comics. 'Are these mine? I always thought she threw them away.' He did a double take. 'Wait, is this one signed by—?'

'Look at the cover date, Marvin.' I tapped the cover. March 1995. Bam. Dadded.

Marvin set the comics down. Gave me the most condescendingly sad look. 'Oh. Kid. These are definitely mine. If you got them from your mom? They're mine. I left my comics with her before we went to London. My apartment was getting fumig—'

'You went to London in January.'

'Yes.'

'These say March.'

'Yyyyup.' The word ended with a pop.

'So unless you had a time machi—'

'The cover date on a comic is two months after the release date, kid. It's a *pull* date. These comics came out in January.'

I looked down at them. Thought about the other comics in my bag. The ones at home. Thousands of pages. Years of my life wondering. Grabbed the two comics on the table and shoved them back into my bag with a shaky hand. 'She said…'

God, I was embarrassed. Am embarrassed. I took a sip of coffee to cool my nerves.

Set the cup down on a rattling saucer.

'She said they were my dad's comics.' I pushed the words out. Was I crying? I mighta been crying. 'Why would she…?'

Marvin folded his arms. Made, like, a 'huh' noise.

I nodded. Definitely crying. 'Huh,' I agreed.

We sat there, quiet for a while. Me crying. Him just thinking. Eventually he went back to eating his sandwich.

'You want my pickle?' he asked. I think maybe he asked that the first time we met too. I don't think I mentioned it.

I did not want a pickle.

'If my mom didn't want me to know who my dad was, she didn't hafta say. Didn't hafta bring him up. She coulda just said they were her friend's comics. Or hers.'

It didn't make any sense. You lie to deny things. You don't volunteer a lie if you're trying to keep something secret.

'I don't know who your dad is. Angie never said. She didn't seem ashamed. Hurt maybe. Sad.'

I nodded. Didn't have any words left. Or I had too many words. I nodded.

Marvin forced himself to look me in the eye. Put his hand on my hand. And he said to me, 'I don't care about the cricket bat, Patrick.'

And I dunno how I knew. How I know. But I know he was lying.

TWENTY-EIGHT

Greenpoint. Mark's Comics is in Greenpoint. You hafta take the G train to get to Greenpoint. You can't even get the G train in Manhattan. It'll only take you from Queens to Brooklyn and back. And… not the fancy parts.

Or. I dunno. Is Greenpoint fancy now?

It's been years since I took the G. Can't even remember why it was, last time. Something-something-kielbasa-something.

But Sasha's comic store is called Mark's Comics, and it's in Greenpoint, so I took the G train and went to Greenpoint.

It's no Midtown Comics. No Forbidden Planet. Side street. Name and address printed on the awning. Fading. Like the banner at Hyperspace. Couldn't see in through the windows. Old comic posters taped up on the inside. *X-Men. Batman. Walking Dead.*

Opened the door and a little bell jingled. Dimly lit inside. Dingy. Claustrophobic, maybe, if I wasn't used to claustrophobic.

Rows of open comic boxes along one wall for back issues. Valuable-ish stuff bagged and boarded and pinned to corkboard behind them. New stuff, comics and graphic novels, on the opposite wall. Displays and spinner racks in the middle for cards, toys, novelties.

Register at the back. Nobody at the register.

Just two people in the store that I saw. Two kids. Maybe 8? 14? On reflection, those are not similar ages. One sat on a stool in front of a back issue box, rubbing it with an eraser.

Other kid sat in a folding chair off to the side. They were arguing about something. Who's stronger? Who'd win? Spider-Man or Aquaman.

'In the water?' asked eraser kid.

'On the side of a building,' said folding chair. I think probably that was the end of the argument.

'You two work here?' I asked.

Eraser kid looked over and sighed and said, 'I do.' Glared at the other kid. 'Moe's just loitering.'

I couldn't help myself. 'What are you doing?'

Eraser kid rolled his eyes. 'Every time I tell the boss there's nothing to do, she tells me to erase the fronts of the boxes.'

'And does that… do anything?'

'She says it gets a layer of dust and dirt off, but I don't see it.'

I bent down, inspected one of the other boxes real close. Squinted. 'You do this one yet?'

'Um. Yeah.'

I stood back up. 'You're right. I can't tell.'

He shrugged and went back to erasing. Moe said, 'Toldja!'

'You old enough to work here?' I asked.

'Probably not. Boss pays me in comics. Mom said it was okay. Don't think the boss has paid anybody to work here since the Pandemic.'

'She laid folks off?'

'The old man did, I think. He…' Eraser kid paused for a second. Glanced back at the register, then back at me. 'Anyway, I like working here. I have a crazy Pokémon habit.'

'It's true!' said Moe. 'He's psycho for Psyducks.'

I let that one go. 'She here today?' I asked. 'She said she'd be here.'

'Hold on, I'll check,' he said, and then he shouted towards the register, 'SASHA, YOU BACK THERE?'

I coulda done that.

I walked back that way. There was a door to the back. Sasha walked out, grumbling. Had she been napping? She was wearing a Mark's Comics t-shirt.

There was a slogan:

'You wanna go for a walk?' I asked.

I said it like a question before, but I'm genuinely not sure if Greenpoint is fancy now. Every part of New York reminds me of every other part of New York these days. Shiny new storefronts next to graffiti and rust.

Sasha pointed us towards the water and we walked.

'Your dad was Mark?' I asked.

She shook her head. 'My dad's name was Lester. Mark was nobody. A made-up name. I think Dad just wanted to trick people into thinking we were part of a chain.'

I smiled. Nodded. 'Like St. Mark's Comics on St. Mark's? Did that work?'

'Actually, St. Mark's moved to Brooklyn last year, so these days it's more confusing for us than anyone.'

'And it's just you now? And, um, the kid with the eraser?'

'Diego. Yeah.' We stopped for a walk signal. 'Dad used to have a couple kids working for comics when he started out. As a lark. Plus, paid employees. Business was good in the '90s. Now...'

'How long ago did he—'

'Two years.'

'Right. Covid?'

'Yeah.'

'Shit.'

'Yeah.'

'Can I ask how he got started?'

'He made a lot of money in the '80s. He was a day trader. Worked crazy hours. Got out before it drove him nuts.' She paused. Thought about it. '*Nutser*, I guess. He poured all his money into the shop.'

'And the con on Long Island?'

'He loved that stupid show.'

'You don't? You wrote a song.'

'I guess. I love *Rescue Rangers*. But *Regulus*? It's less about the show, I think. More about the people.' We were crossing the street. She looked at me like… I dunno. 'They're the family I've got left.'

I laughed involuntarily. Short. Staccato. Immediately apologized.

Thankfully, she laughed too. 'I know, I know, I know. But they're not that bad once you get to know them.'

'Really?' I asked. 'And how long does that take?'

She shrugged as she walked. 'Twenty years?'

Now we were both laughing. The children of *Regulus*. We reached the end of the road and a strip of green overlooking the water. And a solitary bench.

I could see Bellevue across the East River. Brilliant. We sat.

And she finally asked me, 'What's this about, Pat? You were vague on the phone.'

'Lydia thought you might be able to help me?'

'You said something about collectibles.'

'I have this cricket bat.'

That got her attention. 'The *Shaun of the Dead* cricket bat?'

'Yeah, no, it…' *Shaun of the Dead*'s a good movie. 'No, it belonged to Roland Yates. Guess he gave it to my mom before he died? Or in his will or something?'

She nodded slowly. 'Yeah, okay. I probably knew about that.'

'Can't imagine there's a big demand, but if anybody'd want the thing, Lydia said you'd know.'

'You want to sell it?' she asked. Like she didn't quite believe me. I mean, I was lying. I didn't have the bat. *I* didn't believe me. Also, I'm very bad at lying. But I don't think I'd technically lied yet? That's probably what she was noticing. My technical honesty.

'Maybe,' I said. 'Depending on the price.' And other things. 'Who would I sell too? How much could I get?'

She squinted at me. Maybe she was figuring whether she could get a cut? Or maybe the sun had just come out from behind a cloud.

'I can talk to some people,' she said. 'Feel them out.'

No good. I wanted to feel out the people.

'And how much are we talking about?' I asked. 'Like, a few hundred bucks?'

She took a deep breath. Resigned herself. 'There are a couple guys. They'd pay more than that.'

'Thousands. Really?'

She didn't answer. Like, more-than-thousands didn't answer.

And all I could think was, who the fuck are these idiots?

TWENTY-NINE

Sasha did *not* wanna tell me who the fuck they are. Maybe because she wanted a cut. Maybe because she sensed something was up.

Crap, does she think I killed my mom?

Crap! Do I think she killed my mom?

'A couple guys,' she said. Vague. Does 'couple' always mean two? Does 'guys' always mean guys?

Whoever they were, however many of them there were, they were now my top suspects.

Anybody who'd pay that kinda money? Somebody in the community must know them. Sasha was the big pockets at the con. So, somebody new to the community? Or somebody who fell out?

Marvin didn't know. Pointed me to Sasha. But maybe Marvin just doesn't know he knows. Or I could ask Lydia? No. Marvin. Marvin first. Marvin was my new side mystery. Why did

Mom try to frame him for… me existing?

And what could that tell me about my actual dad?

I called Marvin. Invited myself to his place. He didn't say no.

He lived in Manhattan, thankfully. 6 train. Upper East. It was just getting dark when he buzzed me up. Door was open when I got to his floor. He was waiting in the hall. 'Patrick!' he shouted, a little too close to my face. He welcomed me in with a backslap.

His apartment was the opposite of my mom's. Barely lived in. Recliner. Tray table. Entertainment center. Couple filing cabinets. And that was it for the living room. Kitchen was a kitchen. Door to his bedroom was closed. Maybe his bedroom was just mounds and mounds of memorabilia.

Marvin said something, I think. I was probably ignoring him. 'Nice apartment,' I mumbled.

'Did Sasha help you?' he asked. Then, before I could answer: 'Also, can I get you a water?'

I nodded. 'Yeah, thanks. Water, thanks. Sasha, not really. Sorta. She said there were a couple guys.' I was talking to Marvin's back now. He had gone to get me a glass of water. I do that sometimes. Just focus on the last thing a person asked for and forget everything else that just happened. 'I think she wanted to preserve their anonymity,' I said, as he was walking back.

Handed me the glass. 'Sorry. I thought she'd wanna help.'

I held the glass. Didn't drink. 'I think maybe her store's not doing great?'

'That used to be my store. Every Friday, for a long time.' For a second, Marvin was gone. Lost in his head. Before he caught what I was saying. 'You think she's holding out for a cut?'

I shrugged. 'Maybe. Does that sound like her?'

Marvin thought about it, really thought, gestured over to the recliner for me to sit. 'Maybe. I don't get people sometimes.'

I sat and the recliner immediately reclined. I splashed water on my face. Dropped the glass on my chest. Sturdy glass. Landed with a thunk. 'Little help!' I gasped.

Marvin ran around and pushed the recliner back up. 'Sorry. I meant to fix that.' Took the glass, said he'd go get me a towel, went into the back. Bathroom?

I got up. As long as he was in the back, I figured I should snoop. Detective work! I went over to his filing cabinets. Picked one. Opened the middle drawer. VHS tapes. Top drawer. *Yates Pages*. Bottom drawer. Old letters and

He came back with the towel. Bottom drawer is the worst drawer to be caught snooping in. Most crouches are undignified. Butt's just out there.

He tossed me the towel. 'What're you looking for?'

'Um.' Wracked my brain for a good bluff. Settled on, 'I'm trying to solve my mom's murder. Looking for clues.' Shit! That's not a bluff.

Marvin stared for a half-sec and then smiled. 'That's funny,' he said.

I stood and wiped my face half-heartedly with the towel. 'Is it?' I muttered. I don't think he heard me.

'If you wanna look at my stuff, I'll show you my stuff, Patrick. Where do you wanna start?'

He had all of *Regulus* on VHS. And all of *Wonder Grumpus*, Yates' talking hedgehog show. And 'THE' Becky Stratton's episode of *Def Comedy Jam*. Two copies of every issue of *The Yates*

Pages and *The Nil Set*. And all of the original art, correspondence, receipts, bank statements. Everything. Lots of it I'd seen before at Mom's. Copies, I think. That was chaos. This. This. 'This is amazing, Marvin.'

He sat next to me on the floor. Nodded.

'How do you—?' I wasn't quite sure what to say. What I was trying to ask. 'I thought you were like my mom. I was expecting—'

'You expected me to be a hoarder.'

'You *are* still on VHS tapes.'

'I'll tell you a secret, Patrick.' He stood. Waited for me to get up. 'Your mom and I. We *are* the same. Were. Shit.' He winced. Shrugged it off. 'Difference is, every six months I get really sick of myself and throw all my shit away. Everything that doesn't fit in my filing cabinets, or on my bookcase in the back. Or… underwear and whatever. Spoons. Other cut—'

I cut him off. 'I get it. All the extraneous stuff. The stuff you won't miss.'

'Except I do miss it. All of it. Every comic. Every action figure. Every magazine. Every limited-run Happy Meal toy or collector's popcorn tub. But in that one moment in a thousand, I can't. I just. I lose it. It all has to go.'

I've done that. I drew a whole comic when I was ten. It was probably shit. I threw it out with half my bedroom junior year. A poem I wrote about *Star Trek*. My old *Dungeons & Dragons* character sheets. A book report I got an A+ on. It's all gone now. All the reminders of who I was.

It's all just memory now.

'I'm like her too,' I said. 'It scares me sometimes. Mosta the time. Y'know, we got evicted three times when I was growing up.' On reflection, I was maybe oversharing. 'And every time, it it it was this mad scramble. We were days, one time *hours* away from being homeless. I just…' I sniffed back a tear. 'It stays with you, y'know? That insecurity. Like. Like, am I too weird? Too broken? Am I gonna wind up on the street someday like the Maxx?'

'Max?'

'*The* Maxx,' I said. 'Shit, Marvin, they were *your* comics! The homeless guy who hallucinates that he's a superhero in the Australian Outback?'

Marvin shook his head. 'You spent thirty years reading those comics, Patrick. Fixated on them. I read them once, maybe twice, a couple decades ago. *The Maxx* was the Sam Kieth one?'

I nodded. He nodded along to my nodding. Scratched at his moustache.

'Right. There was a cartoon too,' he said. 'On MTV. It was pretty good.'

Might be misremembering what he said. I don't think MTV ever did cartoons.

'Anyway,' he said. 'You're not gonna be homeless. You're a smart kid. You have a nice girlfriend.'

He's never met Lilly. What were we even talking about? Was I a chit-chatter who chit-chats or was I a secret detective?

I took a deep breath. Recentered.

'Talk to me about the Nigel Kent newsletter. *The Nil Set.*'

Marvin nodded. Smiled. Put his hand on my shoulder. 'I can do you one better.'

'Better?'

'How would you like to meet Nigel Kent?'

THIRTY

Nigel Kent. Roland Yates' co-star. Nil from *Regulus*. The man-in-black. *Braddock and Nil met as strangers*. 'Hilariously loathsome' is how I described him in chapter fifteen. His character, at least.

First there was *The Yates Pages*. Then no more *Yates Pages*. Then *The Nil Set*. Then no *Nil Set*.

That Nigel Kent.

Lives in Brooklyn. Park Slope. Good neighborhood. All the trains go to Park Slope. N, R, B, Q, D, W, F, G. 2, 3, 4, 5. That's not all the trains. Mosta the trains. Nice apartment. Doorman. Elevator. Nigel Kent has money. *Regulus* money? That didn't seem right.

Marvin went with me. He's known Nigel for years, of course. Runs errands for him, apparently. Said it would all make sense when I met him. Which I did. And it did.

Marvin knows the doorman, I guess. Waved and walked on by. Up the elevator. Middle floor. He rang the doorbell, and then pounded the door with the side of his fist a couple times. 'Nigel!' he shouted. 'Nigel, open the door!'

I asked Marvin if he'd called ahead. He just stared at me.

And then I heard the voice from inside. Tortured. Hysterical. 'I'm dying, Marvin! They're killing me!'

Marvin frowned. 'Who's trying to kill you, Nigel?'

'The IRS! My nieces!' Nigel moaned through the door. 'That prat from Netflix! The little girl across the hall! Society, Marvin!'

'Society isn't trying to kill you, Nigel. Open the door. I brought a guest.'

'A what?'

'A guest, Nigel. I brought someone to meet you.'

'A physician? Have they come to examine me again?'

'No, Nigel. It's Angie Hinkle's kid. Patrick. Patrick is here to meet you.'

Silence. Marvin looked at me. Half-looked at me. Half-shrugged. Looked apologetic maybe.

Through the door, I could hear locks unlocking. Chains unchaining. Bolts unbolting.

And the door opened just a crack. 'Little Patty? Is that you?'

I could only see a sliver of the man. Tangled gray hair. Gaunt. Bit of mustard in his beard. A faded Mark's Comics t-shirt. *Mark's Comics are your comics!* Pajama pants. Pink bunny slippers.

'Um,' I said. 'Can we come in?' I wasn't sure if I wanted to come in.

He opened the door. It was dark inside. Smelled like my mom's place. Like death, waiting. My mom's, but on a much bigger budget. Book cases strategically placed to block the windows. Piles of papers cascading from every surface down to the floor. Clothes tossed anywhere and everywhere. I counted a half-dozen meals half-eaten, scattered around the living room. Open liquor bottles. Empty liquor bottles. Layers on layers. And underneath it all, some expensive furniture, I think.

And some pee probably.

A projection TV was casting some old show on the far wall. I didn't see the hedgehog, but I'm pretty sure it was *Wonder Grumpus.*

Marvin walked in, walked right past Nigel, started picking up clothes, straightening papers. He turned on a lamp in the corner. Nigel flinched.

'I told you to call me when it's getting this bad,' Marvin lectured.

Nigel mumbled something. Think it was 'Couldn't find my phone.' He ambled over to a couch and swept it clear of papers and pizza and cardboard in one motion. 'Sit, Patty. Sit.'

I frowned at the cushion. Weirdly stained. Sat anyway. I've sat on worse.

'Can I get you anything, dear boy? Juice box? Vodka?'

I said, 'Both of those options seem wildly inappropriate,' and I smiled politely.

He nodded. 'Also, I've drunk all the Vodka.'

It didn't take much to get Nigel talking. And talking. It was a lot, and Marvin was distracting. At one point he was vacuuming. But I've done my best to capture the major points here:

Nigel Kent comes from money. His dad was a lord or an earl or… Maybe both? Can you be both? So he probably had a pretty fancy upbringing. I dunno. Castles and horses and shit.

When he decided he wanted to get into acting, sounds like everybody bent over backwards for him. He played Iago for the Royal Shakespeare Company in '81. In *Othello*, not *Aladdin* obviously. Fuck Disney. He was 26.

When he got *Regulus* a couple years later, I'm not sure if that was a big deal or a big steaming embarrassment for his family. Sci-fi wasn't exactly prestige television back then. Especially in England. There's a show called *Blake's 7* that came out around the same time, and once they had a spaceship that was just two hairdryers.

Look it up.

But the thing is: Nigel was really good in *Regulus*. Even when the special effects and the sets and the model work let him down. Even when the scripts were half-baked. The Nil character was always odious and ridiculous and somehow also cool.

According to Nigel. I've only seen two episodes.

Roland Yates was a comedy guy. His dramatic stuff had swagger, but was mostly overblown. Fine for what he was doing, but hardly elevating the material. Also according to Nigel.

Yates was the star. The hero. When his Braddock and Nigel's Nil went head-to-head, it was always Braddock that came out on top. Yates got the fan club. Nigel and Yates hated each other. Famously went out of their way to antagonize each other on set. Never did appearances together if they could help it.

After *Regulus*, Nigel went back to the theater and worked pretty steadily in smaller productions. Never did any more filmed work. Came to the United States in the mid-90s to do a play off-Broadway and never left. Bought, yes bought, the Park Slope apartment.

The play did not go well. Nigel kept forgetting his lines, snapping at the director and the other actors. After a few weeks of that, he got fired, and nobody else wanted to hire him.

Thing was, Nigel's brain was falling apart.

Nigel didn't say that part, but

What Nigel said was, 'Those shits wouldn't know talent if it fucked them with a Tony.'

And then he shouted at Marvin that he was Windexing too loud.

Nigel had money. He didn't need to work. Coulda sold the apartment and gone home years ago, but he just… stayed.

Marvin and my mom knew him a little bit. From convention appearances. And the London trip, maybe? Marvin would come by the apartment. Help him out. Errands, chores. Sometimes Nigel would try to pay him.

'I don't need the money,' said Marvin. He was gathering up dirty dishes now and taking them to the sink. 'I have a job.'

Nigel frowned. 'He hasn't always had a job.'

Mom and Marvin weren't talking after *The Yates Pages* folded. Nigel said *The Nil Set* was his idea, a plot to get the two of them back together, but I could tell from the way Marvin was shaking his head he disagreed. Anyway, it worked for a little while. Marvin and my mom had a new project. The community was excited for a new fan club and a new newsletter. Somewhere to send their songs and stories and fan art again.

And Nigel, of course, loved the attention. Loved that it was all about him now and not Yates.

The Nil Set made it eleven issues, quarterly, 1996 to 1998. That's the year Roland Yates died. A few weeks after that year's con. Hyperspace 10. Mom's last. My third, a-fucking-parently. She and Marvin did a couple more *Nil Sets* after that, but I guess maybe her heart wasn't in it anymore? And Marvin wasn't gonna do the newsletter without her.

Mom hand-delivered the last issue to Nigel. Teary-eyed. Apologetic. And then she was gone.

Twenty years went by and Nigel just got weirder and stranger. Some years he'd go to Hyperspace. Some not. Eventually they asked him to stop coming. There was an incident. He pooped somewhere he wasn't supposed to. The fans might have forgiven him. 'Oh, that's just Nigel being a rascal!' But the hotel did not.

'Nincompoops,' Nigel bristled. 'Nin. Cum. Poops.'

He hasn't left his apartment in a few years now. Allegedly. Since before the Pandemic. He's survived on delivery and Marvin's goodwill.

I wonder.

Was he one of Sasha's 'couple guys'? He had the money. What would he pay for Yates' bat?

Or was he mad enough to take it?

THIRTY-ONE

I just got back from Jane's funeral. She jumped off a fucking bridge.

THIRTY-TWO

Lilly's not doing well. I've tried talking to her, but she just can't. So I've been mostly staying out of her way.

I didn't know. Still don't really. There's whatever's in front of you. Your life. And so many million other things happening all around you. Everybody else. Their lives. Their stories. If I was open to all that, I think I'd go mad. Maybe that makes me selfish. Maybe I get a pass, because my mom was murdered.

But it was always too much. For me. For Mom.

I guess it was too much for Jane.

Could… Could my mom have killed herself?

No. That doesn't make any sense.

I'm trying to remember when I first met Jane. She was just Lilly's friend at work for the longest time. Like, 'My friend at work had the funniest take on *Game of Thrones*.' or 'My friend at work had the weirdest paper jam!' Whatever it was, it was always the most. The biggest. The worst. Like her life, Lilly's friend-at-work's life, Jane's life, was just *more* than the rest of ours.

I think it was the double date. Lilly tried to set Jane up with a guy she knew from the gym. I think his name might have been Jim? They called him 'Jim Boy' when they were talking about him, like he was a good old boy from Kentucky. But as I write this out, they were probably just calling him 'Gym Boy,' weren't they?

He was an hour late, Gym Boy, and he was wearing his gym clothes when he got there. We were at a nice restaurant. Thai, maybe. He had gotten caught up in his workout, he said. It smelled true. He joined us for dessert, and he was actually kinda funny. He had this dirty Pokémon joke that I can't remember the punchline for now, but it involved a hooker and a half-dozen Jigglypuffs.

It was not enough to save him.

'Worst date ever!' Jane proclaimed.

To his face.

Lilly stopped trying to fix Jane up after that, but I'm pretty sure Jane wasn't the problem.

At least that time.

Trying to remember what else I know about Jane. We did karaoke a few times. Her go-to song was 'Fever.' Which. Fine. But zero points for originality. I don't even have a go-to song though, so I also get zero points. Only Lilly has points. She has, like, seven. It's enough.

One time, Jane was supposed to come by the apartment. Lilly and her were gonna go out clubbing or something. Jane showed up early, while Lilly was still getting ready, and I had to entertain her in the living room.

She looked nice. She always looked nice. She had this kinda style to her, like barely controlled chaos. She did a thing with her hair where she pinned it all up in a way that made it look like it could topple down at any moment.

Precarious. She had precarious hair.

Lilly was taking a long time. Jane and I were sitting quietly. Awkwardly. Just realizing in the moment how little we had in common. How little we had to say to each other. How little our lives touched each other.

She looked nervous. I always look nervous. My leg was vibrating like it does when I sit still. At some point I mumbled, 'Your plans are for tomorrow night, yeah?'

And she just burst out laughing. And she was laughing and I was laughing and I thought, Great! I did a thing. And then her laugh just devolved into this snorting, horrible ugly-cry. And she had this dark make-up on and it was all just sliding down her face, and I wasn't sure if I was supposed to touch her shoulder. Sometimes Lilly touches people's shoulders when they're upset, but my hand just kinda hovered over Jane's.

And then Lilly came out, half-dressed. Top half of her dress unzipped and hanging down. I could see her bra. The gray one. Not comfortable. One eye done. She was pointing at me with her eyeliner, like 'What did you do?' Except she didn't ask, because she didn't wanna hear the answer, whatever it was. Whatever she was imagining.

And she called Jane over and she gave her a hug and neither of them cared what they looked like and, you know, fair. But they were a mess. Kinda just one mess in that moment. And Lilly and Jane went into the back and didn't come out for hours. I wasn't sure what I was supposed to do. It felt weird to turn the TV on, so I didn't. At one point, I got hungry so I made popcorn and probably I shouldn't have done that.

They were noisy kernels.

I dozed.

They came out around two, I think. Jane had redone her make-up. And her hair. Less precarious. Lilly was in PJs. They were gossiping about some guy from work. He was the hairiest. Whatever storm had come had passed. For a little while.

They hugged and Jane left and Lilly glared at me. 'Popcorn?'

I tried to make my shrug apologetic. I don't think it worked.

'Is she okay?' I asked.

'Yeah,' said Lilly.

'What happened?' I asked.

And Lilly frowned. Put her hands in her PJ pockets. They had pockets. Those were great PJs.

And she said, 'Some things you don't get to know, Pat.'

THIRTY-THREE

'Who's the prat from Netflix?'

It was something Nigel said. Part of his paranoid delusion. Everybody was out to get him. His nieces. His neighbor. That prat from Netflix.

Marvin and I were eating hoagies on the floor of his apartment. I suggested that he buy a table and some chairs. He said he threw out the table and the chairs, because they were just surfaces to set things on.

I felt that.

'His name's Douglas,' said Marvin. 'He was at the con. You met him.'

'Did I?' If I did, I didn't remember. Which didn't mean I didn't.

'He was at the diner where you...' Marvin mimed face-planting into pancakes.

'Huh.' I remember remembering that there was somebody

else there. In chapter twenty-one. When I was writing chapter twenty-one. Writing things down is helpful.

'Why was he there?' I asked.

'He was drunk and hungr—'

'I mean, why was he at the con?'

'He's been talking about doing a revival,' Marvin explained, 'for a couple years now. He was talking to Alfie about it.'

'Alfie?'

'Alfie Norton. The genie guy.'

'Genie guy?'

'The guy who wrote the genie episode.' Of *Regulus*. I remember that people were very down on that episode. There's a line from Mom's song. *And one genie we won't dwell on tonight!*

He was a guest at the con. Alfie was. Not the genie.

'Did I meet *him*?' Alfie. Not the genie.

'No. He left after his panel. Well, he had dinner with the Netflix prat, and then he left. Flew back to LA.'

'But Netflix prat we had pancakes with?'

'Douglas. He's okay. Too clingy, people say.'

'And he wants to bring the show back?'

'He says that,' said Marvin. 'People were more excited a couple of years ago. Nobody really knows what he does at Netflix. He could be a janitor.'

'Do you think he's a janitor?'

'No, I think he's a senior executive, but I also think he's too clingy probably and he's not bringing the show back.'

'But he took a meeting with Alfie Norton?'

'Yeah. We all give Alfie a hard time. Genies shouldn't be in outer space. But his career's on the upswing after all these years.

Lydia says he wrote three episodes of *Bridgerton*. Second season, but still.'

'So maybe something *could* happen?'

Marvin balled up the wrapper to his sandwich. 'I don't know, Patrick. Lotta things *could* happen. Somebody could walk up to me and gimme a million dollars. The Mets could win the World Series.'

Fuck the Mets. Seriously.

I tried to summarize: 'So he's clingy and maybe he's rich and he wants to bring back *Regulus*. He's a fan? You think he'd wanna buy my cricket bat?'

Marvin got up, presumably to throw his wrapper out. Grumbled. Might have actually said the word 'grumble.' Which, if so, nice. Walked to the kitchen.

I had to ask. 'You don't want me to sell the cricket bat, do you?'

I couldn't see his face. I could see his shoulders slump.

'What's the deal with this cricket bat, Marvin? Why do you care so much about it?'

He didn't turn around.

'Marv?'

'On the London trip, Patrick. I fucked Roland Yates.'

THIRTY-FOUR

'It was our last night in London.' Marvin handed me a beer. I didn't want a beer. I took the beer. He took a swig of his. 'We had a six a.m. flight the next morning. But this was gonna be the big night. The night we were gonna go see Roland's show. Go backstage. He was doing *Cinderella*. The pantomime. Do you know what a pantomime is?'

I did not. 'Like… charades?'

'No. It's a…' Marvin frowned. 'That's funny. No, it's hard to explain. It's a play, an English play, for children. But also there's alotta adult humor for the… adults. They always do them around Christmastime. They're played very broad. They'll get a c-list celebrity and put them in drag.'

'Right. Yates played the Fairy Godmother?' I remembered the photo. Chapter nine.

Marvin nodded. 'It was *very* camp. No. No, that's underselling it.' He smiled. 'It was gloriously camp. He was… It was like watching *Rocky Horror* performed live.'

'Y'know, *Rocky Horror* started out as a liv—'

Marvin snapped, 'You do not need to tell me the history of *Rocky Horror*, Patrick.'

I apologized.

'Roland brought the house down. Stole the spotlight from everybody. Cinderella. The Step-Sisters. Buttons the Butler. He had this song that was Mae West meets Ethel Merman meets… well, Roland Yates! It was fantastic. It was also maybe not what your mom expected.

'We didn't know who Roland was gonna play until we got there, and Angie's vision of Roland was always… very straight. Macho. The leading man. And this was not that. But I think she came around by the end. And, anyway, we were gonna go see Roland backstage! That was the real event.'

I couldn't remember. 'Had you met him before?'

'Yeah. Few times. Small moments. At the con. Same as everybody. Ang had the Anthem. "Is Angie Hinkle in the audience?" he asked. Like he didn't know. This wasn't in London. This was, what? '87 maybe. At the con before the first Hyperspace. In Jersey City. "Is Angie Hinkle in the audience?" He invited her up on stage and gave her a hug and she nearly passed out. And then he sang her song.

'So, yeah, we'd met. Exchanged letters. He sent me his cricket scores every couple months to run in the newsletter. But London was the first time since starting the fan club that we really got to spend time with him. We were both buzzing.

'An usher found us after and took us backstage. Roland was still in full drag. He gave us both a big hug and a kiss on the

cheek, and he got his make-up on us. He laughed. Ang was…
uncomfortable.

'Also, I had a photo of his face on my shir—'

'I know,' I said. 'I saw a photo.' Chapter nine.

'He made a joke. Something like "You have my head on your
shirt. Does that mean I get your head?" By which he m—'

'Oh God, I get it. I get it.'

'I got it, too. Ang didn't. I blushed. He was testing
boundaries. Told us to wait where we were while he got changed,
and he'd take us out for drinks. For drinks! Out on the town with
Roland Yates!'

I had to ask: 'Marv, were you *into* Yates?'

'Yes.' No hesitation. 'We both were. It was… I was in a real
bad place when I discovered *Regulus*. It was my junior year at
NYU. I was this weird, closeted kid in the mid-80s. I was always
depressed. Terrified of getting sick. I didn't have any friends. I
was drunk one night, late, flipping channels. Wound up on PBS
somehow, and they were airing this ridiculous show. So cheap.
And I don't know what it was…' He closed his eyes. Took a
breath. 'In that first episode, the crew see how they're gonna die.
They see their future selves dead on that spaceship. And it scares
them. That sense of hopelessness. That they can't escape their
fate. But it's also… freeing, I think? If that's their fate, if that's
out there waiting for them, then they can do anything. Be who
they want.'

I remembered the line from Mom's song. At the con,
somebody was wearing the words on a t-shirt. I sang them: '*We
never lived till we died.*'

Marvin nodded. 'That's a quote from the show. Miggsy says

it in the episode "Bonfires Beyond Your Fondest Horizon." I felt that, Patrick. Deep down, I felt it. And Roland was…' Marvin took a long, long swig.

'Was?'

'I don't know. He was the leader. The biggest and boldest. Lotta people liked Nil more. He was funnier. Cleverer. Is that a word?'

He was onto his second beer. Third, maybe?

'Roland took us to a pub. Kept buying rounds. Told us told story after story. Some of them we knew, others we didn't. But we laughed at every punchline. Hung on every word. At the end of the night, we were all wasted. He put Ang in a cab and took me back to his hotel, fucked me, sent me back a few hours later. Ang had already passed out. I thought maybe she wouldn't remem—'

'And did she?'

'The alarm clock went off at four a.m. We both woke up with massive hangovers. Everything hurt. We packed in the dark. No talking. Talking hurt. Caught a cab to Heathrow. Almost missed our plane. Just before we boarded, Ang turned to me and she said, "You did, didn't you?" And there was a look in her eyes. Just total contempt. I've never seen anything like it.'

I had. In a Long Island parking lot. *We. Can't. Afford. Donuts.*

'That was it. The end of *The Yates Pages*. And the end of our friendship. Except it wasn't, because a year went by, and I talked her into coming back to do *The Nil Set*. I put her in a room with Nigel. He can be very charming. Sort of. And I thought maybe we'd gotten past—'

I knew this part. 'But Yates died.' Chapter fifteen.

'We were both torn up.' He set down his beer. 'But that fucking cricket bat.' The man sneered. Fucking sneered. '*I* was the one who loved cricket, Patrick. It was me and Roland! Our thing.' He beat his chest. I took a step back. 'He'd send me his scores for the newsletter. Me. That bat was *for me*, Patrick. It was supposed to be mine. But his fucking estate didn't wanna give the bat to the gay boy, didn't want the implication. So they sent it to *her* instead.' He picked up his bottle. Flung it across the room. It smashed against his TV. Cracked the screen. Beer ran down into the crevices of his entertainment center.

He grabbed me by the shoulder, fingers dug in, this crazed look in his eyes. Hadn't seen that look since the con. Chapter eighteen. And he cried. His whole body shuddered. Buried his chest in mine. He fucking whimpered, 'Please. Please, Patrick. Please don't sell the cricket bat. It's all I have left of them.'

THIRTY-FIVE

I mean, that's more or less what he said. I read some of these chapters back, and I can't always remember which parts people definitely definitely said and which parts I'm filling in. I'm trying, but I can't remember every word in every sentence, can I?

Shit. What if I'm collecting clues in this journal, and the clue is something I filled in. Fuuuuuuuck. Anyway. More evidence that Marvin didn't kill my mom: He was sure I still had the bat. I had to tell him.

'Marv, I don't have the bat.'

He was still crying into my shirt.

'Whoever killed her. He took the bat.'

I think his crying slowed about then.

'I'm trying to figure out who killed her. Who took the bat.'

He took a step back. Wiped his eyes and his nose with the back of his arm in one long gesture. Snorted, and I think they probably heard it down the hall.

And I asked him, 'Would you like to help me catch her killer?'

He stared at me. Tilted his head. Tried to form words.

'Marv?'

He reached out his hand for mine. Slowly. I took it with two hands. That seemed like the right number of hands.

'It would… It would be my privilege,' he said with a shaky voice.

And he looked at me. And I looked at him. Annnnnnnnnnnnnnnnd he was crying again.

Maybe I was crying too.

The next day, I brought him the journal. This journal. Sat down with him on the floor by the recliner, because tables and chairs are just surfaces to set things on. And I let him read it. The whole thing. Not this chapter. I hadn't written this chapter yet.

This is the chapter that I'm writing now.

'Why did you stop there?' he asked. You remember where. It was just a couple pages ago. 'Why didn't you include the part where you ask me to help?'

I didn't have a good answer. 'Sometimes writing everything out is a lot. The chapters break where they break.'

'Is this a chapter?' he asked me. 'What's happening right now?'

'Yeah, no,' I said. 'I'm not gonna write this part down. This is boring.' Shut up. I changed my mind.

'This is a lot to take in,' he said. 'Alotta feelings and memories. Your girlfriend's father. Your childhood. Jane!'

'I know,' I said. 'I dunno. Sometimes it just comes out.'

He put a hand on my shoulder, looked me dead in the eye,

and said, 'Hey. Patrick. You're not a bad kid.'

Maybe it woulda been okay if Marv was my dad. Unless you're Marv reading this. In which case: Be cool, dude.

Later he asked, 'Do you have suspects?' But I wanted his opinion.

He stroked his moustache. 'I dunno. Most of these people I've known for years. It's hard for me to imagine any of them as a killer. But if I'm just going off what you wrote? Sasha, maybe. She wanted to sell the bat because her store's losing money? Or Nigel? You're right. Nige is nuts. Netflix prat, maybe. Douglas. Motive… unclear. Maybe he wanted to buy the cricket bat, but Angie wouldn't sell?'

I shook my head. 'Mom definitely woulda sold the bat. If somebody offered her enough money?' I knew it. I knew it in my soul.

Marv did not. 'I dunno, Patrick. I wouldn't have. Lydia wouldn't have. What makes you so sure your mom woulda parted with Roland's final gift to her?'

'Because she tried to sell it before.'

THIRTY-SIX

It was a Saturday. Early. Mom was supposed to be at work, but instead she woke me up. Got me on the train. She had the cricket bat with her, so I didn't argue or ask questions.

It was still dark when we got there. Ronkonkoma Station. And a Dunkin' Donuts parking lot. Just a few blocks from the hotel. From Hyperspace Con. Saturday morning. Shit. It musta been the weekend of the con. Just a few hours before the first panel.

Hyperspace 12? Hyperspace 13?

She musta gone to meet up with somebody going to the con.

She told me to hold back. Hold the cricket bat. Hold it so people could see it. Fuck. I wasn't her bodyguard. I was her goddamn display model.

I was six? Seven?

Man came, still blurry in my memory, and they were arguing. For real arguing. With spittle and finger stabbing and now and then she'd point at the cricket bat, and they'd get louder.

And I remember. I remember it now. He shouted at her, 'YOU CAME HERE TO SELL ME A CRICKET BAT!'

Which is a weird thing to yell at somebody, but also it seems pretty unambiguous.

Anyway, it didn't go well. He threw up his arms. Stalked off. Back to the con. She stormed past me. Said, 'We're going.'

And I said, 'Aw, can't we at least get a donut before we go?'

So yeah. I'm sure she woulda sold the cricket bat.

But who to? Who was he? The blurry man. Her mystery buyer. Was he the one who killed my mom? Did he remember that she had the bat? Twenty years later, did he decide he wanted it after all? But he didn't wanna pay for it?

Was it Nigel Kent?

Nigel had the money. Mighta even wanted the bat. He was watching Yates' old hedgehog show when we visited. He probably secretly misses the guy. But he wouldn't have negotiated for the bat. The way he is with Marv? He woulda given Mom whatever she asked for.

All the donuts.

The Netflix prat, then?

Douglas from Netflix. No, not from Netflix. Not back then. Douglas from Someday Netflix.

Marv says we met at the pancake diner. But all I remember is a blur.

Marv didn't know Douglas' last name, but he knew who did. Lydia keeps all the mailing lists and shit for the con. Shit shit. I didn't wanna talk to Lydia. I really hurt her when I pretended I wanted to sell the bat. If I came around now, asking for a buyer's last name…

But Marv had a plan.

'Tell her the truth?' I asked.

That was not Marv's plan.

We showed up at Lydia's door without calling. Marv maybe has boundary issues. He knocked. She answered. She was wearing a homemade *Regulus* t-shirt. Nigel Kent as Nil in sharpie, rubbing his hands and saying, 'I'm not plotting anything.'

Me and Marv were plotting something.

Lydia frowned at us, tried to shut the door. Marv stuck his foot in. 'The kid wants to apologize,' he said.

I nodded. 'I'm not gonna sell the cricket bat, Lydia.'

I'm not sure she believed me. She tutted. Opened the door. 'Okay,' she said, and we went in.

Lydia lived in Queens. E. F. R. Not far from my mom's apartment, but muuuch nicer.

Hers was more grandma than I expected. Floral wallpaper. Old, quilted furniture with the curvy edges. China cabinet full of… china. Lotta little tchotchkes everywhere. But, like, classy tchotchkes. Hand carved birds and porcelain elephants and shit.

Nothing *Regulus* in sight except her shirt.

She invited us to sit and Marv did.

'Uh, can I use your bathroom?' I asked.

She pointed me towards the back.

And Marv asked, 'Do you have any of that good tea left?'

This was the plan.

While Lydia went to the kitchen, I went to the bathroom. Went to her bathroom. Flipped on the light and closed the door. From the outside. Her bedroom was the next door down. I felt bad before. About the lying. This did not make me feel better.

Walked in. Sat down at her computer. Her screensaver was, like, a hundred kittens in a pile. I'm a monster. Shook the mouse. Password prompt. Shit. Obviously. Fine. Old people always write down their passwords. I opened her desk drawer and rummaged. Markers. Pens. Sewing kit. Packs of Kleenex. Pad of Post-its, all blank. Buncha business cards that read 'Lydia Mathers, TrueLock Consulting, Internet Security Solutions.'

So. Um. Probably I wouldn't find her password written on the back of an envelope.

Heard Marv bellow from down the hall, 'I DUNNO, LYDIA! HE LOOKED A LITTLE GREEN ON THE TRAIN.' And I could hear Lydia's footsteps. Shit.

And now she was knocking on the bathroom door. 'Are you feeling okay, Patrick? Would you like some tea?' Shit shit.

'Patrick?'

And. Okay. This is the part where I did something stupid. Something really fucking dangerous. If you're a little kid, do not do this. Also, sorry for my language. Anyway, I'm not dead obviously. I'm not, like, a ghost writing this. So don't worry. But also worry a little, because that makes it more exciting.

Anyway, I looked around. It was a nice day. Window was cracked open. I crept over and slid the window all the way up.

'Patrick?'

I told you things were about to get stupid.

'Patrick, if you don't say something, I'm coming in!'

I checked. The bathroom window was open a crack too. So I climbed out. One foot on the sill. One foot swinging in the wind. One hand on the window frame. One stretched for the bathroom window. Stretched till the tips of my fingers reached the window's edge.

'Last chance!' she called.

'DON'T COME IN!' I shouted. As loud as I could. In the direction of her bathroom window. 'I'M NOT WEARING PANTS!'

Please, I thought, please let her be a conservative woman.

And then I fell.

It was a second-floor apartment. It was fine. I mean, it was *not* fine. It hurt like fuck. I landed in the bushes. Scraped and bruised. Little bit of bleeding. Just lousy with prickers. Swallowed the pain. Held back the startled yell when I fell. Held back the pain-pain-ow-ow yell when I landed. But the grunts! Through clenched teeth. Very grunty. Sorta rolled-fell-flopped out onto the sidewalk. Picked myself up. Little wobbly. Glared at a woman walking her poodle. She yipped at me. The poodle did.

Took a second to catch my breath. Think think think.

Had an idea.

Stumble-ran back to the lobby. Buzzed her apartment. Over and over and over again.

'What?!?' she snapped after the sixth or seventh buzz. I don't blame her. I have been terrible to this woman. Genuinely terrible. I need to like, give her one of my kidneys or something.

Both kidneys, maybe. Can you do that? You probably can't do that.

And I said to her, in my best/worst New Yorker accent, 'Lady, I gots a package down here for youze, and youze gotta sign for it. I'm on the meter, *capisce?*'

'A package?' she asked. She wasn't buying it. 'From whom?'

From whom? Is that right?

'Uh, the package says… Um…' Thinkity think think. 'It's says…' Think. 'It says True Lock Consulting. You wannit or what?'

For a second, she didn't answer. And I thought maybe I'd blown it. What do I know? Maybe that place folded years ago and the business cards were just, like, work memorabilia. But then she called down, 'All right, all right. I'll be down in a minute.'

I bolted. Hoped I'd bought Marv enough time for… whatever Marv was gonna do.

Ten minutes later, he found me at the subway station. He was laughing to himself. A good sign.

'What happened?' I asked.

'She was ready to bust in, pants or no pants, so I spilled some tea on her carpet. That bought you a minute to set up your delivery man bit. Good job with that. But Lydia was seething. I took the stairs out while she was on the elevator back up. Texted her that I was taking you home.'

'And sorry about the carpet?'

'Probably I should also apologize for that.'

'And what about the file?' I asked. 'You figure out her password?'

'Password?' He slapped me on the back. Pulled a folded piece of paper outta his pocket and held it up. 'Kids! When I said files, I meant her file-files. Her filing cabinet. I got what we need.'

I laughed, and I gave Marv a hug. He didn't exactly hug me back.

'Um. Don't take this the wrong way,' he said, 'but you look a little fucked up.'

THIRTY-SEVEN

I'm not sure about the odds on this, but there were three Douglases who went to Hypercon this year. Like, is that alotta Douglases or did we get off easy?

Neither of us wanted to do the calls, so we flipped a coin. I lost. Fuck tails. I called Doug One. 'Hi,' I said. 'Is this Douglas?' It was. 'And, uh, do you work for Netflix?'

He hung up. So either he wasn't the guy, or I'd just really irritated the guy. Way to narrow it down, Patrick.

Marv took the next call. Doug Two. Did better. Kinda cheated. Said, 'Hi. This is Marvin from the con. You remember me?' He did, apparently. 'Yeah. I got pretty blotto that Saturday, and now I'm trying to remember something. Did you come out with us for pancakes at the end of the night? Uh huh, uh huh. Okay. It musta been the other Doug. Okay, thanks.'

He hung up. Frowned. 'Just do that,' he said.

So I tried. Called Doug Three. 'Hi,' I said. 'This is Patrick.

From the Hyperspace convention? Not… Not from the convention. At. I was at the convention. I was… I'm not staff, I mean. So. Um. Do you remember me?' He did not. 'Oh. Okay. Well. I was very, uh…' I looked at Marv. He gave me the thumbs up. Why did he gimme the thumbs up? 'I was very, um… *blotto* on Saturday. Do you know what that means?' He did not. 'Right. Nevermind. But that Saturday. Do you remember us, um, hanging out?' He did not. I hesitated. Brief pause. Not sure why he didn't hang up. That's the moment when I woulda hung up. *I* wanted to hang up. I wanted him to hang up. Nobody hung up. Inexplicable.

'There was a diner,' I specified. 'We were at a diner. With Marvin Casiano? Do you know him?' He did. Of course, he did. 'Okay, okay. Great, great. Maybe the three of us were there and—'

'And you passed out in your pancakes!' said Doug Three. With such pure and utter joy. Fuck those pancakes. 'Yeah, yeah. I remember you now. You're Angela Hinkle's kid. Henry.'

'Yeah, no, I'm—' I looked at Marv. He shook his head. 'Yes,' I said. 'I'm Henry. Henry Hinkle. It's just, uh, I don't remember alotta that night, so Marv wanted to reintroduce us.'

'Uh. Okay,' he said. Whatever exuberance was in his voice before was gone. I'd flattened him. 'We're reintroduced.' I looked at Marv. He shrugged.

'And,' I said, not really sure how I was gonna finish that sentence. 'And I… wanted to hear more about your idea to revive the show?'

'Oh, well why didn't you say so!' That's all he needed to hear. Dude cackled. Who passes up an opportunity to hear themself talk? 'Why don't you come by the office tomorrow?'

The office, the New York Netflix office, is just a couple blocks off Union Square. Good location: 4, 5, 6, L, N, R, Q, W. Outside's not much, but the inside might as well be a starship. All white and glass and curves. Douglas' assistant met us at the front desk and took us back.

According to his office door, Douglas was a Senior Vice President. Of something, presumably. In my experience, you're always a Senior Vice President of Something-or-other.

But the door was vague.

Douglas stood up from his desk and smiled. Waved us over to his window view.

Douglas looked nothing like I remembered him. Or. Okay. What I remembered was nothing, so he looked like... not nothing. How old? Forty? Fifty? Tall. Messy gray hair. Probably expensive messy. Suit. Tie. Whatever. He was a guy. People all look the same to me.

I needed to know if he killed my mom.

'Cool view,' I said. It wasn't. Probably. I didn't look. 'You serious about wanting to bring back *Regulus*?'

He invited us to sit. We all sat.

'That's the dream,' he said. 'New show, Netflix budget, maybe co-production with the BBC. Big, modern special effects! Name actors! A whole franchise with spin-offs and licensing deals. Toys! Lunch boxes!' His voice was rising as he spoke. And his hands were... I dunno what his hands were doing. Like, he was conducting an invisible Netflix orchestra.

He stopped. Deep breath. Clasped his hands together. Looked at us. 'Can I get you boys anything? Coffee? Soda?'

'I'll take a Diet Coke,' said Marv. I asked for a coffee.

He buzzed his assistant and said, 'Bring me all the caffeine, Norbert.'

Norbert brought us all the caffeine.

He laid out his big plan for us. Marv checked out a little bit. He'd heard this part before. A relaunch, not a reboot. The great Nigel Kent returns as an older, craftier Nil, now the mastermind behind an interstellar criminal empire. Nil is desperate to break the time loop that'll lead to his death, so he's cloned his old crew, as babies for some reason, and scattered them across the galaxy to grow up and become their own people. Now they're grown and he's gathering them together, to send them back in time to die in his place. But they discover that they're being manipulated by Uncle Nil and decide to change their fate. Steal the ship, go on the run, with Nil and his criminal empire in pursuit. Until they're done running and they decide to take the bad guys down once and for all.

A whole new cast, obviously. Besides Nigel. Douglas said he's talked to Ryan Gosling about playing Clone Braddock. I'm skeptical. And he figured Miggsy could be all CG with somebody big doing the voice. 'Imagine Meryl Streep!' he said.

I cannot.

'And Alfie Norton could showrun. Bring that *Bridgerton* heat.'

'*Bridgerton* Season 2 heat,' said Marv.

I dunno. It's not the worst idea. Hinging it all on a plot point from an obscure forty-year-old British show is a weird choice, but if you could slip it in without too much exposition? Yeah. Yeah, maybe it'd work.

But also maybe this guy killed my mom for a cricket bat.

So I asked him, 'You a collector?'

He frowned maybe. 'A *Regulus* collector?'

'Yeah.'

'There's not much to collect.'

'But if there was?'

'Are you trying to sell me something, Henry?'

'Original props and such.'

'There's no market.'

I nodded. 'Maybe after the reboot?'

'Relaunch.'

'After the relaunch?'

I could tell he didn't wanna answer, but whether it was because I was on to him or because I was just really annoying him with my rapid-fire questions, I dunno. I changed the subject.

'How long have you been a *Regulus* fan?'

Douglas shrugged. 'Few years. One of my guys showed me a tape. Cool stuff.' And he looked at Marv. 'How long have I been coming to Hyperspace?'

'Four, five years?' Marv guessed.

'Sounds right. Good peop—'

'Why Nigel Kent?'

'Excuse me?'

'Why center the reboot—'

'Relaunch.'

'—relaunch on Nigel Kent?'

'What can I say? Some folks are Braddock guys. I've always been Team Nil.'

'And you've met the man?'

'We've spoken.'

'He's nuts.'

'Who isn't?'

'Hasn't performed in thirty years.'

'Maybe he deserves another shot.'

'You know one time he pooped in a…' I glanced over to Marv.

'In an ice machine,' said Marv.

'Really?' said me.

'Two times,' said Marv.

'Jesus,' said me again.

I had meant to catch Douglas' reaction. I did not catch Douglas' reaction.

Douglas stood. Looked at his watch. Apologized. 'It's been nice catching up, gentlemen, but I have a Zoom with the cast of *Squid Game* that starts in five.'

No time. What did I wanna ask him? Did you kill my mom? For a cricket bat? Twenty years after she tried to sell it to you in a Dunkin' Donuts parking lot?

Were you blurry back then?

All those questions and more and the thing I managed to blurt out was 'Were you at Hyperspace Con in 2002?'

He stopped. Looked at me. Squinted. And said slowly, 'I said I've only been to Hyperspace the last four or five years.'

'Technically Marv said that. You just agreed with him.'

He said, 'I'm sorry about your mother, Henry.' Gave me a Top Five death stare. Top Three. And then he left us there in his office.

Marv sipped his Diet Coke. I sipped my coffee. Chairs were comfortable. Nobody was rushing us out. We had a think. A minute or so of that and the first thing I said was 'I really thought he'd be phased by the poop thing. Didn't you think he'd be phased by the poop thing?'

'It's been fourteen years, Patrick. I'm *still* phased by the poop thing.' Marv set down his coffee mug. He had a different thing he wanted to talk about. 'Did he say he was *always* Team Nigel?'

I wasn't sure. But Marv was, so that's why I wrote that he said that earlier.

'It's a weird thing to say,' Marv said, 'if you've only known about *Regulus* for a few years.'

I agreed. And there was something else. 'Yesterday. When we were on the phone? He said, "You're Angela Hinkle's kid." Like he knew my mom.'

'I dunno, kid. Your mom cast a long shadow.'

My whole life, my mom *was* the shadow.

I finished off my coffee with one last swig. Doug Three from Netflix knew about the poop. Was always Team Nil. Knew my mom, maybe?

'I think he was there,' I said. 'Back then. I think he's the guy.'

I just didn't know how to prove it.

On the way out, we passed Norbert the Assistant. Young guy. Good energy. I asked him, 'What exactly is your boss the Senior VP of?' And also I thanked him for the coffee. After that. Always, always the wrong order.

'Yeah, um.' I'd confused him. Probably I also shoulda said hello first. Or goodbye? He was at the copy machine. I'd interrupted. I apologized, which I don't think made him less confused. Behind me, I think Marv shrugged. Or gave some other nonverbal clue that I was harmless and to be humored.

Norbert looked past me at him. Then looked at me. At him. At me. Shrugged it off.

'Human Resources,' he said. 'Doug's the Senior VP of Human Resources.'

THIRTY-EIGHT

'Motherfucker doesn't even work in the entertainment division!'

I said that. Marv said, um, *something* in response. I didn't hear it over the roar of the uptown R pulling into 14th Street Station. Probably it was, 'Right on, Pat! You're the best.' Or probably not that.

We got on the train. 'Can we go back to Lydia?' I asked. 'Do her con records go back to the early 2000s? The 90s?' Not that I wanted to. I was tired of lying to her, but worried how she'd take the truth.

Marv shook his head. Sat. 'No, she only keeps the last seven years. It's a compliance thing.'

I slid down next to him. 'Also, she hates me. She hates me, right?'

That was where Marv coulda said something like, 'No, Pat! You're like a son to her. Also, the thing I said earlier is that you're the best.'

He did not say that.

We sat in silence for the rest of the ride mostly. Marv almost said a thing, then didn't. There were some breakdancers. The breakdancers aren't part of this. They were just there. They were pretty good, but I didn't know the song they were dancing to.

'*The Nil Set*,' said Marv, as we were getting off at 59th Street. 'If he was "always" Team Nil? I bet he was on our mailing list.'

And that motherfucker was. Fuck. And he was on *The Yates Pages* mailing list! Right back to the beginning. Except he wasn't Douglas back then. He was 'D.G. M——.'

Marv swore as he went through the paperwork. 'I remember that little shit.' We were back at his apartment. Marv was pulling everything he had from his magic filing cabinets. Not just the mailing lists. He opened up a manilla folder and handed me a photocopy of a hand-typed short story, 'Braddock and Nil and the Bondage Planet.' It was dank stuff. Alotta leather. Lotta chains. More throbbing than seemed strictly necessary.

'And you published this?' I asked, quietly horrified.

'No,' said Marv. He snatched it back from me. 'He sent me dozens of these across the two newsletters. Years of this shit. I was always very clear with him. From the beginning. Nothing that would make the stars uncomfortable. And his shit? It just kept getting worse and worse. Listen to this!' He flipped through another submission and read aloud, "Their lips trembled with expectation. Their thighs quaked. Their hot, sweaty peni—'

I cut him off. 'I get it, I get it. You ever meet him back then? As D.G.?'

Marv couldn't be sure. 'It was a long time ago, Patrick. And there were a lot more of us back then. I didn't know everybody by name. Alotta people introduced themselves. Maybe this guy was too shy? Too… too weird, maybe?'

I nodded. 'A weirdo, hanging out on the edges of fandom. You don't know him. Maybe Mom does? He has money. Mom doesn't. Maybe he wants the cricket bat?'

Marv mouthed the words 'cricket bat' and swore. Dropped the short story. Riffled through his files. 'Yeah, yeah. Shit. We published one thing he sent in. One thing, one fucking time! A letter.' He pulled a copy from a folder and read: '"Dear Editors, Thank you for including Roland's cricket scores every month. As an Anglophile *and devoted cricket fan—*"'

I grabbed it from Marv, the letter, half-crumpled it in my hand. Held it up to him like shit-we-got-him. And. I dunno. I remember swearing a lot. Maybe just shouting noises. And Marv was shouting and swearing and spitting and saying what he was gonna do to Douglas when he got his hands on him. Which I wanna stress was all very normal legal non-murdery stuff, because the next thing that happened was that the phone rang and JESUS FUCK it was loud and

And I just wanna say. The odds that I actually have my ringer on are so unbelievably small these days. It was very confusing. I didn't mean to answer it.

It was the police.

I said, 'I'm sorry, officer. We'll keep it down.'

That was not why they were calling. The woman on the other end said, 'It's about your mother, Mister Hinkle. We'd like you to come down to the station.'

THIRTY-NINE

The detectives met me at the elevator. Marilyn and her partner. From chapter five and, I don't know, ten or whatever. Oh! And her name actually is Marilyn. I thought I'd made that up.

Maybe this shitty journal is more accurate that I thought.

Her partner's name definitely isn't Marilyn though. The babyface detective. He's got a little wisp of a moustache going now. It's not helping. His name's Stuart-something. Or maybe something-Stuart?

It's possible Marilyn is Marilyn's last name.

These are not important details.

Anyway. They walked me back to Marilyn's desk. They had her chair and a couple more pulled up so we could all sit. I looked around. Phones were ringing. Cops were… copping.

'I guess whatever you need to tell me isn't too private?'

Marilyn frowned at me. Sat. We all sat.

She leaned in. Put a hand on my knee. Had an expression on

her face. I didn't know what was happening. Didn't like it.

Detective Stuart said, 'They caught him, Mister Hinkle. The Van Nuys Pants Bandit. In Van Nuys. He confessed to… um…' He looked to his partner.

'Sixteen murders,' she said. As calm as anybody'd ever said those two words in that order.

Detective Stuart nodded. 'Right. Sixteen. But not your mom's. He has an alibi for the night she died. He was delivering pizzas. In Van Nuys. He's not the guy.'

After he was done saying that, the two of them just stared at me for a while. I think Detective Marilyn mighta still been touching my leg? I don't remember. I think they were waiting for some reaction: Disappointment. Sadness. Anger. Fear.

But I didn't feel anything about the Van Nuys Pants Bandit because I never thought he was the guy. I'm pretty sure D.G. Douglas M——— the Netflix Prat is the guy. I had the letter he wrote crumpled and folded up in my pocket. I wanted to tell them. Explain what I've been doing these last few months. All the clues. All the dead ends. About Douglas being a Human Resources slash-fiction-writing cricket-enthusiast liar obsessive shitbag murderer.

'It's right here,' I'd say. And I'd show them the piece of paper from my pocket. 'You see? He's an *Anglophile.*'

They'd think I was insane. Shit. I probably am insane. Do you know how much my hand hurts from writing all this shit out longhand? What is wrong with me? Lilly, if you're reading this and I'm dead, it's because Marv and I are gonna go confront Douglas. Shit. Sorry. Other stuff happened at the police station. They asked me to tell them about the night she died again.

Maybe they think I did it now?

I answered their questions, I think. And then I left. Went home. Called Marv.

'Are we doing this?' I asked.

'Motherfucking shit yeah we are,' he said. Which meant yes.

And I wrote that down. It just happened, so I'm very sure that's what he said.

And now I'm gonna leave this journal here, right here, on the ironing board and, yeah. Lilly, if you're reading this because I never came home, it's because Douglas from Netflix killed me.

FORTY

So it turns out I'm not dead. Currently.

Marv and I walked straight past lobby security. Zero eye contact. Straight to the elevator. When we stepped out, we remembered/saw the big glass wall and the door that you need a keycard to open. But it was end of the day, so we just waited till somebody was walking out and we walked in.

Ocean's Eleven's got nothing on us.

Lady at the front desk smiled at us and said, 'Oh, you're back? Let me ping Norbert.'

Now, we'd been walking at a brisk pace. Sweat was dripping. Adrenaline was pumping. Marv had a grimace on his face that was… unsettling. I had been reflexively clenching and unclenching my fists.

Lady pinged Norbert. I woulda called security. Not sure why they didn't call security.

Minute later, Norbert walked up, backpack over one

shoulder. 'Hey guys!' he said. All cheery. What is wrong with these people? 'Doug's finishing up a call, and I'm on my way out. Can I set you up in a conference room? Maybe get you some snacks? Maybe show you where the restrooms are if you need to wash up?'

I wasn't mad at Norbert. Norbert radiated youth and guileless charm. Norbert didn't kill my mom. But, no. I did *not* wanna wash up.

I ran. Fast as I've ever run. Panting. Half-stumbling. But fast half-stumbling. Across the office. Open floorplans absolutely suck unless you're trying to clear the distance from the front desk to the VP's office before a half-dozen HR managers can tackle you to the ground.

Nobody knew what was happening, but they knew it was weird and, God bless them, they were trying to stop it. Marv was right behind me, running interference. Clotheslining people. Shoving them into desks.

We were bad people.

I collided with Douglas' door. Hit it hard enough I cracked the frosted glass. Also maybe my shoulder. Behind me, it was chaos. Everybody was shouting or, um… weeping, maybe? I mean, fuck. Had nobody had ever stormed the Netflix offices before?

They're turning *Squid Game* into a game show for God's sake.

And Douglas. Douglas swung his door open with the biggest scowl on his face, and he had his Bluetooth headset on and he was mad enough that maybe he forgot he was in the middle of a call and he got as far as 'What the f—' before he saw me and he saw Marv and he saw the look in our eyes and he turned and fucker ran. Back into his office, vaulted over the desk, foot caught on the monitor cord, twisted, slid, head knocked into his office chair, flopped awkwardly over the far side and outta sight, dragged the monitor after him and it sounded like maybe it bounced off his head.

Me and Marv entered. Marv shut the door. Muffled the chaos. Probably now they were calling security.

I shouted, 'We know what you did, Douglas!'

And I could hear him behind his desk, and he'd lost it. Absolutely lost it. Sobbing. Pleading. 'I'm so sorry! P-Please! Please don't hurt me.'

I really didn't think it was gonna be this easy. But also good, y'know? It'd been a long year. I got out my phone and swiped to my voice recorder app.

So for this next part, for once, I know *exactly* what was said:

ME: Why'd you do it, Douglas?

DOUGLAS: Oh god oh god, don't don't don't. I didn't I didn't plan it. I just I hated them all so much. All of the. They were they were supposed to be my people. My my crew. But they treated me just like everyone else did. Like like a dirty little freak. Like I I I didn't belong. The misfits didn't didn't want me. So I left. Left and got my life together. Grew up. Came came back. And and and oh god it was an accident, I swear. I didn't I didn't mean to—

ME: Say what you did, Douglas.

DOUGLAS: Marv Marv asked where I worked so I said said said Netflix and everyone was so impressed. Paid attention to me. Listened. Not like before. It's it's all I ever wanted.

And I didn't want that to go away. So I so I told them I was relaunching the series. I'm so sorry, Henry! I don't even know Ryan Gosling!

VOICE ON HEADSET: [inaudible]

DOUGLAS: You're right. Sorry, Larry. I'll I'll go on mute.

I stopped the recording.

FORTY-ONE

The last time I saw my mom alive was a few months before the Pandemic hit. She'd left me a voicemail message, texted, and when that didn't work, she sent me an email. The email said check your texts. The text said check your voicemail.

The voicemail said, 'Patty, I think the thing under the sink is gonna kill me.'

Just those words, flat, and then she hung up.

I called her back immediately. Obviously. And by immediately, I mean however long it had taken me to check my email, then my texts, then my voicemail. A few days probably. Maybe a week. I dunno. I'd been busy, okay? The Dragonhold DLC had just dropped for *Elder Scrolls Online*.

Anyway, I finally got the message and I called her and she told me there was a smell coming from under the sink. She thought it might be Death.

'It's not Death,' I told her. 'Death comes through the front door.'

I came through the front door. An hour later I knocked and she opened the door and, oh God, was she right about the smell. Mom's apartments always smelled rank, but this was next level. I took a step back, out into the hall, buried my nose in the crook of my elbow and asked, 'Mom, what is that shit?'

She was crying and shaking her head. 'I dunno I dunno I dunno.'

I pulled her out into the hall. Told her to wait there.

There was a CVS a few blocks away. Bought some nose plugs. Rubber gloves. All the cleaning supplies. One of those grabber toys with a plastic robot hand on the end.

When I came back, she was slumped down in the hallway, opposite her door, staring blankly. If I couldn't see her breathing, I mighta thought she'd died then and there. God, she looked old. She was fifty-four. Looked so much older. Hair a greasy gray, long and tangled. Skin wrinkled with worry and regret. Back bent. 'What am I gonna to do?' she whispered.

'Nothing,' I said as I walked up to her. 'You never do anything.'

I put in the nose plugs. Put on the gloves. Went back in. The smell was definitely coming from under the sink. I mean, the worst of the smells. I crossed the living room into the kitchen, reached out with the grabber arm and slowly opened the cabinet door below the sink.

The smell wafted out like an acid fog. I recoiled. Shoved the door shut with the grabber. But not before I saw the thickest coat of black mold inside. I dropped the grabber, got out of there. Told my mom we had to go and took her back to my apartment.

This was when I was still living with the potheads. Before I'd moved in with Lilly.

Our apartment wasn't much better than hers, but it wasn't that.

I made her take a shower. Made her a coffee. Sat down with her on the couch.

'It's not safe, Mom. You gotta call the building people to take care of that.'

She grumbled and avoided eye contact. 'If they see what the apartment looks like, they'll kick me out.'

'Kicked out is better than dead.'

'I'm not gonna find another place, Patty. I'll be out on the street.'

I sorta hrmmed to that. Notably, I didn't offer for her to stay with me.

What I did offer was to clean for her. Enough that she'd feel comfortable having somebody from the building come and inspect. For them to bring somebody in to do mold abatement.

But before all that, I sent her home. I know I know. I dunno.

I mean, it'd been like that for however long. How much worse could another few days be?

I showed up the next day, a Tuesday. Took the day off and cleaned. And the next day. And the next. Sometimes big projects like that overwhelm me, but if I can just keep doing the thing that's immediately in front of me, sometimes I can power through. And I had plenty in front of me:

Put my nose plugs in. Did the laundry. Did the dishes. In the *bathroom* sink. Gathered up trash and took it out to the dumpster. Scrubbed every surface in the apartment but under the kitchen sink. I plugged the drain. Ran duct tape all along the cabinet door. Bought a can of air freshener and sprayed the shit out of that apartment.

Thursday night, the place looked halfway livable. Smelled like industrial chemicals, but looked halfway livable.

The look in her eyes. Like I'd done something amazing, when all I'd done was get her back to base-level human. I gave her a hug. Left the cleaning supplies. Said maybe I could come by once every week or two to help her keep it up.

Made her call the building people while I was still in the apartment with her.

That was the last time I saw her. Before she died.

Except we Zoomed once. March 2020. Two or three weeks into the lockdown. It took about an hour on the phone to talk her through the set-up for a five-minute video call. Turns out she'd never used the webcam I'd ordered for her, and she wasn't sure where to plug in the headset.

'You're not going outside, are you?' I asked when we finally got connected.

She said something, but she was on mute. I told her she was on mute. Told her how to get off mute. Several times.

'Just once or twice,' she said. 'To get groceries.'

'No,' I said. 'Stay inside. I'll set up grocery orders for you. Tell me what you need. And I'll send you some masks! Stay inside. Don't talk to anybody.'

She nodded meekly. 'That's mostly what I always do.'

'Can you still work?' I asked.

She shook her head. 'Bookstore's closed. Restaurant's closed. Some of the accountants are working remotely, but I haven't... I think they're gonna let me go.'

'Well, I don't think they're kicking anybody out of their apartments right now. You should be okay for a while. Till everything is back to normal.' March 2020. 'People are saying maybe it'll be done by Easter.'

'How is that woman?'

'Lilly? Good, Mom. Lilly is good. Lilly's good in a crisis.' I wasn't sure if I was gonna tell her, but I told her. 'We're talking about moving in together actually. Mostly on account of the Pandemic. They're calling them Pandemic pods.'

I don't think she was following me. She said something, maybe asked a question, but she'd muted herself again.

'You're muted!' I shouted. I dunno why I shouted.

She unmuted. Repeated, 'I should meet her soon. If you're gonna live in sin together.'

I squinted at her. Her face was lifeless. Expressionless. Was she joking with me?

'Yeah,' I said. 'Soon.'

Soon.

FORTY-TWO

I skipped work again today. It's been… a while since we stormed the Netflix offices. Couple months, I think.

Part of Douglas not getting fired was him convincing everybody that we were doing a very small flash mob. I guess word got out, because it's… sorta a thing now? The other day there was a very small flash mob at Lilly's work.

'It was the smallest,' said Lilly with a tear in her eye. 'Jane would've loved it.'

I was so sure it was him. When it wasn't, I just

I've been sleeping a lot. But at the wrong times. Playing *Elder Scrolls Online* in the middle of the night on the European servers. They keep kicking me out of their groups because I get distracted during boss fights. Not falling asleep. Just… losing focus.

Been binging coffee and junk food. Fingertips are orange with Cheeto dust.

When I close my eyes, I see her face. The zig-zag impression the carpet left on her skin. That dark stain she left on the carpet, like a hole in the universe.

I've been throwing up in the afternoons, when Lilly's at work.

Marv's called a bunch. Even Lydia. I've been deleting all their messages. I don't wanna know.

I bought the Billy Joel album with 'Piano Man' on it. It's called *Piano Man*. I've been playing it on loop. Next track after 'Piano Man' is called 'Ain't No Crime.' Fuck you, Billy Joel. That's the song we danced to after we all sang the Anthem at the con.

Chapter twenty, maybe? Whatever.

I sleep on the couch a lot. The bathroom floor sometimes.

Fuck, I don't wanna be homeless. The Maxx hallucinating Australia.

Lilly's been reading more comics lately, which isn't something I'd normally mention or maybe even notice, but a few hours ago I set down my glass on the ironing board and I saw a Mark's Comics bag.

Mark's Comics are your comics!

Lilly was somewhere else in the apartment. I called out to her, 'Have you been going all the way to Greenpoint to get comics?'

Toilet flushed. Minute or so later, she stuck her head in. 'Yeah,' she said. 'I like Sasha, and her store's not doing great. We can't order everything from Amazon all the time.'

I mean, technically we could order everything from Amazon all the time.

She walked over, pulled a graphic novel out of the bag. *Mister Miracle*. 'I thought you might like this,' she said. 'It's really bleak.'

Or she said something like that. I was still looking at the bag.
And something in my brain
Something in my brain
'Oh,' I said. 'Of course.'

FORTY-THREE

I showed up at Mark's Comics a few minutes before closing time. It was already getting dark. And cold. Blustery. I was underdressed.

Sometimes the seasons sneak up on you.

Diego was there, the kid who erases comic boxes, behind the counter, ringing up a customer. I didn't see his friend. Or Sasha. I flipped through the back issues till the customer left. Jimmy Olsen was a giant turtle man for some reason.

'Sasha here?' I asked.

She was not. 'She left a few minutes ago,' said Diego. 'Said she was going for a walk.'

'She left you to close up?'

Diego shrugged. 'I turned fourteen last week. She says I'm ready.'

I wondered whether he was standing on a crate behind the counter. Not important. I asked, 'Do you know which way she went?'

'She likes the water,' said Diego.

I found her on that bench, looking out across the East River. In a heavy coat, drinking a coffee. I shivered as I approached her. 'You clearly know what the temperature is!' I said. Instead of hello. Then I said hello.

She didn't turn around. She took a sip of her coffee. Said, 'Hi, Pat.' I swear I've only met this woman twice. Three times, now.

I asked if I could sit and she said okay, so I sat. She looked over at me and laughed. Just a little. 'Is that a windbreaker?' she asked.

I crossed my arms, pulled them tight. 'It's not breaking much wind tonight.' After a second I added, 'That… wasn't supposed to be a fart joke.'

She turned back to the water. Took another sip of coffee. Smiled. Asked, 'When did you figure it out?'

Like I coulda sat on it. 'Today. Earlier. A couple train transfers ago, I guess. They should really maybe move Greenpoint somewhere closer. It was the bag.'

'Yeah?' she said. She didn't understand.

'One of the things that never made sense to me is why my mom would lie. She held onto a bunch of Marv's old comics and told me they were my dad's. She never even told me about Marv.' Sasha nodded along to my explanation. 'Why tell me they were my dad's comics if they belonged to Marv?'

'It's weird sometimes, what people won't let go of.'

'Because they *were* my dad's comics. Once. Like it says on the bag: "Mark's Comics are your comics." Marv's comics were

Mark's comics.'

She turned her head to look at me. Wiped away a tear. 'It was always a stupid slogan.'

'Lester was my dad, wasn't he? You're my sister.'

She smiled. Sniffed. 'You remind me of him a little. The way your brain works.'

'I met him once,' I told her. 'Sorta. In a Long Island parking lot. Years and years and years ago. Mom wanted to sell him the cricket bat. He musta come there wanting to see me. He was so angry when he realized.'

I remember it now. 'YOU ASKED ME TO MEET YOU?' he shouted. 'DRAGGED THE KID OUTTA BED AT FOUR IN THE MORNING?' Maybe. 'AND YOU'RE TELLING ME YOU CAME HERE TO SELL ME A CRICKET BAT?'

Or maybe that's just my imagination filling in the blanks.

'She must've really needed the money,' said Sasha. 'Way Dad told it, there wasn't anybody your mom loved more than Roland Yates.'

'We always needed the money,' I said. 'I guess you had a different mom?'

'You a detective?' she asked, very fake-impressed. Sasha's Black. It wasn't a big leap. 'Your mom and my dad were only together a little while, but that was it for him. Just meaningless affair after meaningless affair after that. My mom was…' She peered down into her empty coffee cup. 'Well, she was someone else's mom.'

'But you knew? About me.'

'He'd talk about you sometimes. "You know, you have a brother out there." Wondered what happened to you. Not sure if he lost track of your mom or just couldn't bear looking for her.'

'Why didn't you say anything? When we met at the con. Or last time I came to see you?'

'I don't know, Pat. You're like him, I think. I loved my dad, but I could never really rely on him. He was always off in his own world. Off in outer space. Anxious. Depressed. But always dreaming. About that ship. That crew. All those crazy adventures.' She shook her head. Almost smiled. 'Which, okay, it was a lot of fun when I was little. But it got so much worse as he got older. He got worse. The real world couldn't hold his attention the way a forty-year-old television show could. He forgot to pay the bills. Stopped listening to me in the middle of me talking. Always had seven things to say for everything I said, and could never wait till—'

'I always thought it was my mom,' I said. 'Everything that's wrong with me. I thought it was because of her.'

She nodded. 'Parents, right?'

'You didn't kill her,' I said. A statement, not a question.

'Did you…?' She sorta squinted at me. 'Did you think I did?'

'I dunno. Not really, I guess. It's just… I've been trying to make sense of it, you know? Figure out what happened.'

'I get it,' she said. 'Since Dad died, I've been trying to make it make sense too. 2020 was…' A tear rolled down her cheek. 'So many people were dying. Every day. Did you know they built a makeshift morgue on the street outside Bellevue? Right across the water.' She pointed. She didn't need to point. I remembered. 'That's why I started coming out here. To this bench. To this view. That's where they took him, after he died. Into that fucking white tent.

'Tent's gone now. He's gone. City's moved on. Everyone expects us to move on too. Take our masks off and pretend it never happened.'

Her eyes were red and puffy. Her face, slick with tears. I was probably crying too.

I'd always thought that he'd come back some day. My dad. Like King Arthur rising from the dead in *Camelot 3000*. To save England. To save me. But King Arthur wasn't coming back.

England would hafta save itself.

We sat in silence for a little while. I watched my breath trail off into the night.

Fucking windbreaker. I shivered. Stood.

'I should go,' I said.

'Okay, Pat.'

'I'm gonna go,' I said. And I turned. Headed back toward the subway.

'Pat!' she called after me. I'd walked maybe twenty feet.

I turned back. Shivered in the wind. 'Yeah?' I said.

'My dad,' she said. Not shouting, but loud enough for me to hear. 'A few years before he died, he got an ADHD diagnosis. Some drugs. It helped a little.'

FORTY-FOUR

Lydia buzzed me in. I was last to arrive. Which was fucking embarrassing. Sure, the N train was delayed coming out of Manhattan, but also 'THE' Becky Stratton had flown in all the way from Toronto.

Also also, this was all my idea.

I hafta give Marv credit. I was dubious when he suggested Nigel host. But Marv did a real top-to-bottom number on the place. The apartment was spotless. He'd moved the shelves out of the way of the windows to let the sun in. Turns out Nigel has a balcony! He cleared out the trash. Scrubbed or dusted every surface. Both, when appropriate. Dishes done and put away. Laundry done and put away. All Nigel's papers, filed away or recycled. And I'm happy to report that the couch cushions were stain-treated and now smelled pleasantly of nothingness.

Soft, boppy jazz was streaming through speakers placed strategically throughout the apartment.

Poor Nigel seemed dazed by it all. He just sorta milled around, guest to guest, asking if anybody needed ice.

They were all there. Even the people I didn't expect to come. None of them needed ice.

After she buzzed me in, Lydia sat back down with Marv. They were reminiscing over the contents of an old manilla folder when I came in. Lilly had found Cousin Joan. They were sharing pictures from their phones and laughing like old friends. Worrisome. Douglas from Netflix was in the corner with his assistant Norbert, dictating an email to All@Netflix.com. Something about keycard security. Sasha and Diego were out on the balcony, enjoying the view. Well, Sasha was. Diego was complaining about the unfinished CGI in the new *Ant-Man* movie. Eileen, who always won the Hyperspace Costume Contest, was showing 'THE' Becky Stratton the lacing on their show-accurate cosplay boots. Nihal from the bodega called out, 'Hey, Sugar Man!' when he saw me. I don't remember inviting him, so I guess Lilly must have? Probably shoulda explained my plan better. Older woman, very put together, was studying the framed photos on Nigel's wall. Old theater cast photos. Musta been mom's old boss-secretary, Evelyn.

And the detectives were there. Marilyn and Stuart. Whispering in the corner. Flipping through their tiny notepads. Stuart's moustache was filling in nicely.

I made sure to say hi to Lilly first. Kissed her on the cheek. Thanked her again for her help getting everybody together. Cousin Joan smirked and said, 'You know a number of interesting characters,' which... fair. Marv and Lydia showed me a photocopy of a particularly egregious D.G. slash-fiction story from back in the day, which I immediately took over to show Norbert. Douglas snatched the story out of his hand before he could read it, protesting, 'I'm in HR now!'

Went over and gave 'THE' Becky Stratton a hug and thanked her for coming. And complimented Eileen on their boots. I let them tell me that they were season two boots, even though I could tell that by looking at them. I've seen all of *Regulus* three or four times now.

It's growing on me.

Went to the kitchen and got Nigel a glass of ice cubes as a gag. Found Evelyn and thanked her for coming.

'It's strange,' she said. 'I've been thinking a lot about your mother recently.'

Me too.

Gave the detectives a thumbs up from across the room. Detective Stuart gave me the nod back. They knew their part.

Other people? Less so.

It was Marv, finally, who stood up and asked the question. 'So, uh…' He did a thing with his phone to turn down the music. Cleared his throat to quiet the rest of the room. Kinda phlegmy. 'I suppose we're all wondering why you gathered us here today?'

'Sorry.' I nodded. 'Yeah. Sorry for being mysterious. I wanted to get you all together to… I wanted to get you all together last Tuesday actually, but "THE" Becky Stratton had a gig. Which is great! Really. Last Tuesday was a year since my mom died. Which you all… You all knew her. Mostly.' I scowled at Nihal. He'd opened a bag of chips. Had he brought his own chips? Nevermind. Focus. Focus. 'You all knew her better than I did, I think. I grew up not knowing about any of you. Not knowing about this huge chunk of her life that she'd given up. It's been twenty-five years since Roland Yates died. Since she walked away from *Regulus*. From all of you. And…

'And I learned a lot, meeting you all. About my mom. About myself. I got answers to questions I've been asking all my life. Answers to questions I didn't even know to ask. But there was one question I still can't answer: Who killed Angela Hinkle?

'I've been looking for her killer, this last year. You maybe heard. Investigating. Keeping a journal. Gathering clues. Identifying suspects. Made some accusations, even.' Douglas grumbled at me from the corner. 'I couldn't shake the feeling that somebody from her past had murdered her.'

That got them fidgeting. Good.

'Lydia,' I asked. 'How did you feel about my mom?'

'About Angie?' She managed a sad smile. 'I loved that woman. She was the closest thing I've ever had to a sister, and I have two sisters!' I'm sure she's told that joke a lot. Nobody laughed.

'And you were never jealous? That she ran the newsletters with Marv? Got to see Roland Yates in London? That it was her song that everybody sings, year after year?'

'Oh, honey, no. No, they worked so hard.' She reached over, patted Marv's shoulder. 'And I had my career. I could never. But your mom especially was so kind, so welcoming. She cared *so* much. You just can't be jealous of somebody like that.'

'Did you feel that way, Douglas?' I asked. 'That my mom was 'so kind, so welcoming'?'

He snorted. 'Not to me, no. Your mom could be very judgmental. Sorry. Very *protective* of the show. The actors. Of

Roland and Nigel. All of them. And she wasn't shy. She told me off. More than once. In public.'

'You musta resented her?'

'Honestly, it was a bit of a turn on.'

'Ew. Moving on.' I turned to 'THE' Becky Stratton. 'Mom gave the guys alotta attention, right? Roland and Nigel. Did you feel overlooked?'

'Overlooked? I don't do jokes about being a little person, but if I did do, this is when I would.' Off-the-cuff. She was very funny. Nobody laughed. 'No, no. Your mum was brilliant. She was genuinely interested in us as people. In my stand-up. Some fans only want the blue face paint and the funny voice, but your mum wanted to know *us*.'

'And you, Nigel?' He was still holding the glass of ice I'd handed him. 'Do you remember the last time you spoke to her?'

'I…' He looked at the glass of ice for a moment. Set it down on a shelf. 'I know my mind's going a bit. That I don't always remember things. Or remember them the right way. But some memories… Your mother, that dear woman. She came to me with a copy of *The Nil Set* in hand. The final issue. And she apologized. Said she couldn't do it anymore.'

'This was after Roland Yates died?'

'Six months perhaps. I'd thought she'd… Well, not moved on, but… Started to make peace with it. But she looked at me, Patty, with tears in her eyes, and she said, "I can't. I'm sorry." And then she walked away. From all of it.'

'Sasha,' I said. 'I know you didn't know my mom, but—'

'It felt like I did sometimes. Dad talked about her a lot. I know he loved her. Missed her.'

'And my mom?' I asked. 'Do you know how she felt about him?'

'I don't. She didn't want to be with him, but she kept those comics, right? He must've meant something to her. Must've been weird between them.'

I agreed. 'The two of them, so involved in the community. He was funding all the cons back then, right?'

'Yeah. They worked around it. For a while, at least.'

'For three years, right?'

'Until Yates died.'

'Give or take.' I turned again. 'Evelyn, Joan, thanks for coming. I wanted to ask you about Mom's email forwards.'

'What about them?' asked Joan.

'Why do you think she sent them?'

Neither of them wanted to answer. 'It's okay,' I said.

Evelyn chose her words carefully. 'Your mother was a very… *lonely* woman. At the time that I knew her. She clearly wanted to make friends, but I suppose she'd lost whatever part of her that you all saw back then. Her sending those emails, it was an attempt to… stay connected.'

'Did you ever reply?' I asked. 'Ask her to stop sending them?'

Evelyn shook her head.

'Joan?'

'*I* didn't. There was a Reply All once. Years and years ago. Before you or Evelyn were on the list. Someone said, "Stop. Just stop." That's it. And I remember thinking: I will never be that brave. Or cruel.'

'And did she take that person off the list?'

'Oh, I don't remember. Maybe.'

I thanked them both.

And now the detectives. 'Detective Marilyn. Detective Stuart. Thanks for your patience. Could you please tell everybody here what you told me when you called last week?'

Detective Marilyn nodded and took a step forward. 'First, we wanted to say thank you for inviting us. It's Stuart's birthday almost, and he's always wanted to do one of these. And I hadn't gotten him anything yet.' She looked around the room. 'Also, um, sorry for your loss.'

'But the phone call?' I prompted.

'Right,' she continued. 'It's like I said. NYPD never officially closes a murder investigation, but there's a point where we've gathered all the evidence. Followed every lead. We've done as much as we can. We may never know what happened to your mother, Mister Hinkle, who killed her, but everything points to a random home invasion.'

'Nine times out of ten,' said Stuart. He looked disappointed.

'Ten times out of ten,' said Marilyn.

'You don't think it's the Van Nuys Pants Bandit?' I asked. More a statement, really.

'No,' Stuart confirmed. 'His alibi's solid.'

'And you don't think she was murdered by somebody she knew twenty-five years ago?' asked Marv.

They did not.

'Then why are we here?' asked Lydia. She looked a little peeved. 'At first I thought we were having a nice dinner party to remember your mom, but then it turned into a whole Agatha Christie thing, and now I'm not sure what's happening. Do you know who killed her or don't you?'

'I thought *I* killed her,' I said. To Lydia. To the room. To myself, I guess. 'For a long time, I blamed myself. When I was growing up, it was just the two of us. No friends. No family. And she was working all the time. And when she wasn't, she was so so tired.

'Before me, she had all of you. And I thought maybe she'd walked away for me. That she had to choose between *Regulus* and me. That the bright, vital woman you all talk about is dead because of me.

'But I don't think that anymore.'

'Then what *do* you think?' asked Douglas.

'She loved the show. All of you. You were her crew. It's like you all said: She was welcoming. Protective. Saw the actors, not just the characters they play. All the actors. Yeah, she loved Roland Yates, but she didn't leave after his newsletter folded. Didn't even leave after he died. What you said a minute ago, Nigel: She brought you the final edition of *The Nil Set* six months after Roland died. *Six months.* She didn't leave because Roland Yates broke her heart.'

I let my words hang in the air for a moment. Just a moment.

'She left because Marv did.'

Marv bolted up from the couch. 'Sorry, what?'

'You almost told me,' I said, 'in your apartment that day. The day you smashed your television set. After he died, the Yates estate sent Mom his cricket bat. But cricket was always your thing, yours and Roland's. It was your idea to run the cricket column in the newsletter. You wrote it. He sent *you* his scores. You told me how you stumbled onto the show all those years ago. It was Roland you connected with. You were a scared, lonely kid, but Roland and *Regulus* gave your life purpose. You were every bit as torn up about Roland dying as Mom was. Maybe more. Probably more. You both loved him, but only one of you had actually been *with* him.'

There were some murmurs from the room. They didn't know.

'Yates, though. He was in the closet. The estate would never acknowledge it happened. Never let a whiff of it out. So a few months after he died, his bat arrived at *my* house. For *my* mom. And when she told you—'

'I went nuts.' Marv snorted back a tear, nodded. 'I was angry as I've ever been that night. Got drunk as I've ever been. When she called me? To tell me? There was this… this brightness in her voice. A joy. And I snapped.

'I went to her house. Your house. Shit, it was pouring rain. Thundering. I was soaking wet by the time I got there and just just just vibrating with rage. I was younger then. Leaner. Tougher. Scarier. And I knew it. I got loud. And she came out swearing. I could hear you crying inside. It didn't phase me. I wasn't about to back down. Roland had *promised me* that bat. That night he took me back to his hotel room. We talked cricket after. In his bed. "Have to find my old bat," he said. "I'll send it to you." To me.' He beat his chest with his fist for emphasis. 'It was supposed to be mine. But Angie kept saying, "If it was supposed to go to you, how come I have it?"

'And we went back and forth and back and forth and the rain was pounding us, and she was kept saying, "How come? How come?" and finally I snapped, and I shouted into her stupid face, "Because you never fucked him!"

Marv took a moment. Tried to slow his breathing. 'And she knew.' His voice was getting shaky. 'I knew she knew. But part of her, even then, wouldn't let her admit it. She snarled at me. She fucking snarled. And she said: "Roland Yates is NOT a f—."'

'I didn't hit her. As mad as I was. As drunk as I was. I knew that if I hit her, I could fuck her up. I-I didn't want that. As mad as I was, I was holding myself back. Because I loved Angie. And, aw, shit. I knew. I knew if I let her push me, I'd do the wrong thing. So instead… Instead…'

Marv rubbed a tear from his eye with his wrist. Wiped it away on his pants leg.

'I said, "You're done." I said, "Keep the fucking bat. I don't wanna ever see you again. I don't wanna hear from you again. You stay the fuck away from me, from the con. You don't call, you don't write. You are fucking done." Fuck fuck fuuuck.'

He slumped down onto the floor. Let his back rest against the couch. His head fell back onto the cushion.

I said, 'She shouldn't have said that.' Softly.

'Of course, she shouldn't have said that,' he said. 'But I… I shouldn't have… She tried to apologize. But I wouldn't talk to her. For months. For years maybe, she tried. I screened her calls. Returned her letters unopened. And then one day, one Friday afternoon, she sent me a joke email forward.

'It was me. The Reply All. My last words to my best friend were "Stop. Just stop." Fuck her, she never did. For twenty years. Every Friday. Until she couldn't anymore.'

We were all quiet. Even Nihal, thank God. Except for Marv, sat on the floor, whimpering into his palms. Nobody knew what to say. What to do. Except Nigel, apparently. He spilled all the ice cubes out of his glass and onto the hardwood.

'Look,' he said. 'An icebreaker!'

Lilly found me later, out on the balcony, as the sun sank below the skyline and the wind picked up. I was underdressed, as usual.

'Well,' she said. 'That was a lot.'

I nodded.

'You don't look happy,' she said. 'You don't look satisfied.'

I shrugged. 'This is just my face,' I said. 'I'm not responsible for my face.'

She sidled up beside me. Slipped an arm around my waist and looked out onto the city with me. Well, Brooklyn. 'You still want to know,' she said softly, 'who killed your mom.'

'I don't have the temperament to solve a murder,' I told her. 'I've been told.'

'Yeah, maybe,' she said, and she hugged me a little closer. 'But I've been thinking about that. About that journal of yours. It's not just your investigation in there, is it? It's the story of your whole life.'

I winced. 'I'm really sorry about calling you Livid Lilly.'

She ignored me. 'There was a moment, do you remember it? At the start of chapter twenty-four. You asked yourself why you were writing in chapters, instead of using date entries like in a regular journal. Did you ever figure out why?'

'No, I...' It still bothered me. 'I dunno. I wrote that whole first part in a day. At the time, the date I wrote it seemed less important than the, uh...'

She waited. Smiled patiently. Till I found the words.

'…than the story I was telling.'

'There it is,' she said. 'In the real world, yeah. You might never know who killed your mom. Or why. But, maybe, *in your story…*'

She reached into her coat pocket. Pulled out a pen. Her best pen. The pen I wrote the first twenty-three chapters with.

The pen that writes upside down.

WHAT SHOULD BE

FORTY-FIVE

They say it can take months to get an ADHD diagnosis. Years. First you hafta find a doctor who's qualified to diagnose you. Who'll take your insurance. Who has appointments open before the next ice age. Wait. Do the assessment. Wait. Get the results. And after all that, you might hafta find a whole other doctor to prescribe medication. To figure out the *right* medication. The right dosage. Trial and error. Trial and error. It took Lester… it took *my dad*… four years to get his diagnosis and figure out the drugs that worked for him.

But I found a doctor who could do it all in a day.

Which either makes him a very good doctor or a very bad doctor.

I think those are probably the only two options?

'Zere are ze different types of ze ADHD,' he explained to me. He talks like that. Doctor Azgore. He's got a checkered bowtie and he smells like weed and his beard's mostly moustache and his office is at the top of a skyscraper overlooking Central Park. He has these huge floor-to-ceiling windows. The view's amazing. Also distracting. I may have missed some of what he was saying. 'When people zink of zer ADHD,' he said, 'ze picture in zer head is often ze rambunctious boy who terrorizes ze zird-grade classroom. Who pulls ze pigtails. Runs with ze scissors. Eats ze glue.'

'That's not me,' I said. 'I hate trying new foods.'

'Yes, yes,' he said. 'Very good. But zere is anozer kind of ze ADHD, more often diagnosed in adulthood, more often diagnosed in ze women, called inattentive-type ADHD.'

'In women?' I asked. 'You're saying that I have what? Lady ADHD?' I tripped over the syllables. 'LadyHD?'

'Yes,' he said. Probably to shut me up. 'Because so many of ze symptoms are internal, because ze symptoms are less *disruptive*, it may not be caught until much later. You're still in your twenties. What a wonderful gift to find zis out when you did!'

It didn't feel like a gift. I always knew there was something wrong with me. Something I couldn't properly explain. Couldn't name. Something other people couldn't understand or quantify. So I had to face it alone.

To give it a name now, it doesn't gimme those years back.

Dr. Azgore's assistant came in to offer me a selection of herbal teas. 'Decaffeinated,' she clarified. The tea bags were fanned out on a tray beside a pink tea cup and matching pitcher filled with hot water.

'I don't like tea,' I told her. 'Also, no thank you.'

When she was gone, Dr. Azgore pulled a small black box

from one of his drawers and set it on the desk between us. Like a pair of earrings would come in. I was pretty sure he wasn't offering me earrings.

'Other people will have other solutions for your ADHD. Systems. Lifestyle changes. Talk zerapy. Zese people are vultures.'

That didn't sound right but also now I wanted to know what was in the little box.

'Zis,' he said, 'is ze new experimental treatment for ze ADHD. Are you prepared?' I nodded, but that apparently wasn't good enough, so he asked again, more forcefully. 'Are you prepared, Miiister Hiiinkle?'

'Um. Yes,' I said. Preparedfully.

He lifted the top of the box. A green light shone from within. It was a pill. A glowing green pill. He held it up with two fingers. 'Very new,' he said. 'Very experimental. We call it ze FocEx.'

'Is that...' I leaned forward. Squinted. Scrunched my nose maybe. 'Is it radioactive?'

He clenched the pill in his fist. The green light seeped out between his fingers. 'Only a little,' he said. 'Perfectly safe. But definitely only take one a day.'

He reached out his hand, so I reached out mine, and he dropped the pill onto my open palm. It was warm to the touch. Glass smooth. And... pulsing slightly?

'And this is gonna help me with my ADHD?' I asked.

'Indeed it will,' he said. 'And more.'

I studied the pill. Turned it between my fingers. 'And more?'

'Effects vary. We are still doing ze testing. Ze studying. Results are confidential. But one of my patients recently developed ze x-ray vision.'

I set the pill down on the desk. 'Excuse me?'

'One of ze side effects is superpowers.'

I looked at the pill, glowing on the doctor's desk. Looked out the window. To gleaming towers. To the city below.

Something had changed in the universe. Shifted.

I placed my hand over the pill. Studied its light between my fingers. Felt its vibration up my arm.

Looked over to Dr. Azgore and said, 'Maybe I will have that tea after all.'

FORTY-SIX

I met up with Marv in Central Park. He'd been jogging. Trying to get back in shape. His sweats were soaked with… sweat.

Oh shit.

Sorry. I honestly did not realize that's why they're called sweats that until this exact moment. Till these exact pen strokes. Just assumed it was because, I dunno, they're made in sweat shops? Which— Double shit. Which are probably called that because the slave labor kids get really sweaty!

Language, man.

Anyway, jogging is the reason that when I walked up to Marv sitting on that park bench, the first thing I said was, 'Shit, Marvin, you stink.' He gave me the finger. Reasonable. He'd lost ten pounds. And a weight he'd carried for twenty-five years. He looked good.

'It's happening,' he said. Grinning. Like I was supposed to know what he meant.

'Is it?' I asked.

'The reboot!' he said.

'Relaunch?' I corrected.

'Whatever. They're bringing back *Regulus*.'

I sat down next to him. 'Who? Netflix? How is that even possible?'

'Yeah,' he said. 'It's a weird story. It turns out that Norbert is the Secret Prince of Netflix, and because Douglas was kind to him, Norbert granted him three wishes.'

'Wishes?'

'Yeah. I don't think he's done the second two yet, but Douglas is an SVP of Content now. He greenlit the reb—'

'Relaunch.'

'And they're going to do three seasons! Mainly because the original ran three seasons and artistic vision something-something, but probably also because Netflix only ever wants to do three seasons of anything. They got Alfie Norton as showrunner off Douglas' original pitch!'

'And the cast?'

'Gosling's a go! Not sure who they're getting for the voice of Miggsy. They're still figuring out how to film around Nigel's theater schedule.'

I clapped Marv's arm. 'I saw him on the side of a bus! Oh my God! Nigel's a parrot!' On hundreds of busses, on billboards, on subway posters. Nigel Kent as Iago in Disney's *Aladdin*. Fucking Disney. On Broadway.

Marv laughed. 'I think he still thinks he's doing *Othello*! I've been too—'

'Parrot *Othello*?'

'I would be first in line for Parrot *Othello*!'

'Can you imagine?' I attempted a croaking parrot voice: 'Out, out, damn spot!'

'I think that's from Parrot *Macbeth*,' he said.

'Shit. Do you know any lines from *Othello*?'

He did not. 'Are you still keeping that journal?' he asked.

'Nah,' I lied. Because it was too hard to explain.

We sat for a little while, enjoying the day. The breeze. Finally, I remembered the box in my pocket, took it out and showed it to him.

'Are you giving me earrings?' he asked.

I smirked and opened it up for him. Just a crack. Enough to let some light out.

'Emerald earrings?'

I sighed. Pulled out the pill. Showed it to him. He said, 'The fuck's that?' And I said, ' I know! It's supposed to cure my ADHD.'

'By making you grow a new head?'

Was 'new head' a superpower? 'Shit, I hope not.'

He smiled. With his whole face. With his moustache! 'Well, that's great, kid. I hope it does the thing you want it to.'

I nodded. 'The doctor said I should take it in sunlight. That's not weird, is it? When I say it, it sounds weird.'

'World's weird these days,' said Marv. Truth. 'Some guy from Maximum Fun Network asked me to do a podcast.'

'About *Regulus*? Because of the reb—'

'Relaunch, yeah. They want me to do it with "TH—"'

'That's great, dude! Now I'm gonna take this magic pill!' And I tossed it into my mouth. Poor impulse control. That's a symptom of the thing I used to have. Before the pill. Marv said my eyes glowed green right after I took it. Just for a second. And then the whole world, it

I don't know if I can

It'd take a whole chapter to catalog every fucking thing that's wrong with me. Everything the pill set right. But maybe I can start with one thing. Two things?

I've talked before about the force field. The thing that holds me back. Maybe less about the other thing. The thing I don't have a name for. The thing that tells me what to do. To go back to sleep. To pick up a game controller. To keep scrolling. To lose myself for hours. Months. *Years*. While a lifetime slips away.

While my mom's killer is still out there.

My whole life, it's been that push and pull. I can't. I have to. I can't. I have to.

Until I took that pill. And suddenly I could do anything I wanted.

I don't mean

Not *anything* anything.

I'm not a genie.

What I mean is I could *want* anything I wanted. I could do the thing I wanted to do.

There was no more 'I have to.' No more 'I can't.'

Just me sitting next to my friend Marvin Cassiano on a bench in Central Park, deciding what to do with the rest of my day. As a jogger jogged by. As a songbird flew overhead.

Whatever I wanted.

And I said to myself, 'Fuck. I wish this were real.'

FORTY-SEVEN

I was home early. I found Lilly in her good PJs, sitting cross-legged on the couch, leafing through a book she'd bought off eBay called *Your Partner Has ADHD*. Her reading glasses had slid down to the tip of her nose.

'Hey, babe!' she said as I came in. She smiled and closed the book. 'You ever experience RSD?'

I took off my jacket. Hung it on the coat rack. Scratched the back of my head. Tried to puzzle through the acronym. 'Rectal… something… disorder?'

'Ew. No. Gross.' In a split-second, her nose-scrunch of happiness became a nose-scrunch of disgust. 'This book says some people with ADHD experience something called Rejection Sensitive Dysphoria. It's a condition where you don't like criticism.'

'Doesn't everybody have that?'

'Sure, but… Like, a lot. I don't know! Read the book!'

'Okay.'

'Okay?' she repeated. In the years we've been together, I've read mosta Lilly's sci-fi books and exactly zero of the self-help books she's recommended to me. 'Okay, I'll read the book,' is the sorta thing Pod-Person Me would say.

I took the book, examined the cover, glanced over the back cover blurb, flipped through the interior pages.

'Don't get distracted!' she warned. 'That's also a symptom.'

I handed the book back to her. 'I'm not. Did you hear that Netflix is doing the show?'

'The *Regulus* reboot?'

I paused. Considered how I wanted to respond.

'Yes.'

'Babe—'

'You keep saying that. You never call me that.'

'I'm trying it out. What do you think?'

'Seems fine.'

'Babe, why are your eyes glowing green?'

I shrugged. Eyes felt fine. 'Doctor said there'd be side effects. Just lemme know if I grow a second head, okay?'

That evening we went to see Nigel in *Aladdin*. I didn't fall asleep once, and Nigel remembered most of his lines. It was a great night for both of us! At intermission, I stepped out into the lobby and checked my messages. I'd remembered to silence my phone before the show started.

There was just one, and it was the police. Detective Marilyn. She said, 'Mister Hinkle. This is Detective Bogdonavich.' Marilyn Bogdonavich probably. 'I don't wanna alarm you, but the man they arrested… the man who confessed to being the Van

Nuys Pants Bandit… He was a crackpot. He was lying. He didn't do any of the murders. We only eliminated the Pants Bandit as a suspect in your mother's killing, because the crackpot wasn't in New York that night. But if he wasn't the killer… Mister Hinkle, the Van Nuys Pants Bandit is still at large, and we think he killed your mother.'

Lilly tugged on my arm and nodded towards a side door. 'Nigel asked if we wanted to see backstage,' she said. So I followed her. 'Who left you a message?'

No point in worrying her. 'Telemarketer.'

My instinct was to delete the message. I'm not my instincts.

Nigel's parrot costume was amazing. A big red feathered costume. Lilly says they don't dress Broadway-Iago up as a parrot, but this is clearly better. There's a hook-and-pully system to fly him around the stage.

'Is that safe?' I asked him. 'You're not a young parrot.'

He shrugged. 'When you get to be my age, Patty, it's not a question of if you're going to die, but how spectacularly you can go out!'

I nodded politely. 'Marv says you're doing the relaunch!'

'It's not a reb—' Nigel started, but then he realized I'd said the right thing.

Somebody knocked on Nigel's door and shouted, 'Five minutes to stage, Mister Kent!'

Nigel stood and lowered the parrot mask back over his head. 'I'll be right there!' he called back. Gleeful. Giddy, even.

And then the giant parrot turned to me and said, 'Oh yes. We start on Monday! Alfie's flying in from Los Angeles! I've read the scripts, and they're wonderful. The kind of nuanced, dignified character work that I've always wanted!'

Said the giant parrot.

He gave me a hug, which he didn't need to do. And one to Lilly, which maybe I'd prefer he didn't? She smiled and said, 'Break a leg!' to him, and he said, 'Indeed, I shall!' before exiting for the stage.

And then it was just the two of us in Nigel Kent's dressing room. Lilly looked at me. I looked at her. She said, 'Should we—?' and I said, 'Snoop around?' and she giggled and said, 'Yes, please.'

Nigel had taped a yellowed press clipping to his vanity mirror. From when he played Iago in *Othello*. 1981. The critic called it 'a promising debut amidst a lackluster production.'

Nigel highlighted the last part. Always the production holding Nigel back.

Lilly pulled the card from a large bouquet of flowers and read, 'From your biggest fans! Good luck, Lydia and Marv.'

'Checks out,' I said. I slid open a drawer and found the script for *Regulus: Resurrection* episode one. 'Babe, come look at this.' 'The Second Act,' by Alfred Norton.

Lilly hung an arm over my shoulders. 'Probably we shouldn't,' she whispered. Which wasn't exactly telling me not to.

I turned the page and read:

EXTERIOR – THE UNIVERSE – FORTY YEARS LATER

CLOSE ON an enormous star, fiery yellows and oranges, as a starship crosses silently, dwarfed by the star, silhouetted by its light, a tiny but recognizable shadow. This is our hero ship. The star is Regulus. The ship, THE REGULUS.

As the ship passes off screen, the title appears in bold white block letters across the star.

Cue the fanfare.

The lights flashed. The signal that we were supposed to take our seats.

The second act was about to begin.

FORTY-EIGHT

Before I moved in with Lilly, I lived with these three brothers. All potheads. For a few years. It was weird being the responsible one.

I wasn't that responsible.

They weren't nice people, but mostly they had their own shit and I had my own shit and mostly that was fine. But there was this one thing they'd do that I absolutely hated them for. Every once in a while, every few months, I'd have dinner with them. Or play a game of cards with them around the table. Share a six-pack. Whatever. And mostly I'd be the one cleaning up at the end, because fuck them, they weren't cleaning shit, were they?

So I'd clear the table, and then I'd come back, and there'd be one thing I'd missed, so I'd clear that, and then I'd come back, and shit there was something else I'd missed, and so I'd clear that, and then I'd come back and motherfucker shitfucker, the sixth or seventh time I did it, I'd realize they were just setting out more and more shit on the table, and I was just reflexively compulsively picking up whatever they set down and clearing it, and those motherfuckers would laugh like this was the funniest shit they'd ever seen.

And it always worked. Always worked. I dunno how many times they did the same joke. Fuckers. A dozen times, maybe? And I didn't know why I didn't know, didn't understand, didn't process any of that. I just did it because I did it because that's what I do. What I always do. The thing that's in front of me.

Just one of the many, many things wrong with me.

There's a thing I read online. Somebody talking about their ADHD. About having ADHD. They said, 'We don't have personalities. We have ADHD symptoms.' We grew up thinking we were weird. We were off. That we were wrong about everything. But at least we were special little snowflakes. Except we aren't. It's embarrassing. Every little quirk, good or bad, everything that makes me me?

I can find it on a fucking checklist on Reddit.

I've been reading the book Lilly recommended: *Your Partner Has ADHD*. Probably I should find a book that's actually written for the person who has ADHD, but this is the book that Lilly left out for me on the ironing board, so I'm reading it.

The main thrust so far seems to be: Your partner is a small, useless child. Everything's terrible, and it'll never get any better. Consider hiring a maid.

Reading the book, reading about other people's experience with ADHD, it has me thinking back over my entire life. Everything that's wrong with me.

I have trouble focusing. Or I focus too much. Can't turn it off. They call that hyperfocus. I can lose a whole day on a game or a wiki or an Excel spreadsheet for work.

I can't. I have to.

I have trouble writing. Constructing thoughts. Except *this*, for some reason. Everything has to be perfect or I can't let it go. And I can never do perfect, so I can never let go.

I try really hard to seem normal. Well, not *really* hard.

Life is exhausting.

Sometimes, if I'm not paying attention and I don't hear everything you say, my brain just makes up whatever it wants to fill in the blanks. And then I forget anyway.

There's the anxiety. Depression. Hard to stay productive. Committed. Every life hack I've ever tried has worked gloriously for an hour, a day, a week maybe. Then nothing.

If a task's too complicated, my brain just shuts down. I need a video game or my phone, and then I'm gone for hours. I'm nowhere. I can't do multiple things at once. I can barely do one thing at once. Except sometimes all I can do is one thing.

I'm repeating myself. I repeat myself.

I like lists. I have so many lists. Everywhere, lists. Grocery lists. To Do lists. Lists of clues. I set goals for myself, but I'm so easily distracted. I'm always doing the last thing somebody told me. I need very concrete steps to get anything done. And maybe somebody to show me first. And maybe second or third.

And even then. I always do the easy parts first. And then I stop.

I hafta explain myself. I need to be understood. I repeat myself. The thoughts in my head come so fast that if I don't blurt them out, I'll lose them. I want people to understand me, but also to like me, which is a problem.

I know I can be overly sensitive, defensive. I hafta try actively to not care. Not caring is how I get through the day. I hafta tell myself. It can't matter. It can't

Sometimes I lose track of what I'm saying and just

Sometimes I make stupid, carless mistakes. Sometimes I'm jittery, even when I haven't had a drop of caffeine. Caffeine helps me sleep. My ideal sleep cycle is 2 a.m. to 11 a.m.

I'm always at eleven.

I know I'm supposed to trim my fingernails more often than I do. And my toenails? Fuck my toenails.

When I was younger, I tried everything. Every hobby you could think of. I guess not every hobby. Some hobbies. Played alotta *Dungeons & Dragons*. Collected several stamps. For a week, I was really into the trombone.

As a kid, I wanted to do the right thing. I wanted be kind, but I was always too quick with a joke. They weren't even good jokes. 'You look like a banana that's not ready yet.' My brain's just faster than my mouth. I wind up interrupting. Blurting things out. Backtracking to say the normal human thing. 'Also, sorry.' 'Also, you're welcome.' 'Also, I love you too.'

Waiting can be agony. In a conversation. Too many things to say. Everything you say, I have five things to say in response. How can anybody keep track of all that?

I get lost in my thoughts. Memories or dumb ideas for sci-fi books or *Star Trek* episodes. Maybe they could do one where the ship's shields are slowly crushing them.

Sometimes I feel like that. Like the invisible walls are closing in.

Sometimes the past comes back and hits me like a hammer.

When I close my eyes, I still see the zig-zag pattern that the shag carpet left on my mom's dead face.

I was a shit son, wasn't I?

The worst thing about video games is when you hafta keep practicing a very hard move until you're good enough to do it one time. Except I never learn. Never get better. I once lost a whole night to *Elder Scrolls Online*, trying to jump my character from one outcropping of rock to another. I forget why. Hundreds of attempts, just waiting to be lucky one time.

My life is just failing till I'm lucky.

I forget to grab a basket at the store. Wind up with my arms full and things falling everywhere.

Sometimes I get so mad and then half an hour later, I can't remember why I was mad anymore. Which maybe sounds nice, but is actually really upsetting. Like I've lost a part of me.

Paperwork is overwhelming, all those applications. Insurance forms. Regular people fill them out without a second thought. I care too much. I don't care. I hafta have a system. Systems fall apart. I hafta do one thing. I can't. I have to. The first thing first. The easy thing. The last thing you said. What did you say? Is what I heard the thing you said? Or the thing my head said you said?

What is any of this? What even am I? What is wrong with me? What happened? What did I do wrong? Why do I repeat myself? Why is everybody normal but me? Why do I sleep on the bathroom floor? Why do the control panels blow up every time the Enterprise gets hit with a photon torpedo? Couldn't they fix that? Are the dragons in Elsweyr lore-breaking? Why why

       why why

why

There's a glowing green pill in a little black box on the counter in the kitchen that can fix me. Fix me. I don't have a personality. I have ADHD symptoms. And if I don't have ADHD symptoms

Being me is awful. Not being me is

I walk to the kitchen. Twenty-three steps. Open the box. Take the pill.

My eyes flash green.

FORTY-NINE

The limo was waiting for me when I got downstairs, just like Douglas said it'd be. It was just a town car, but it was nice. The driver had a complimentary tiny bottle of water for me. In case I wanted to drink a small amount of water.

It was only a twenty-minute drive to the Navy Yard, but Douglas said he was saving me thirty minutes of my life and fifteen minutes of walking, and he didn't even mention this tiny water bottle, so really he was going above and beyond.

Also, it was four in the morning. That was the big downside to all this.

I had asked Marv if he could get me in, and then Nigel if he could get me in, and neither of them did shit as far as I can tell. Douglas reached out on his own. 'Would you like to see us film *Regulus*?' he asked. I said no, I was very busy these days, and he asked if I was joking, and I told him I was.

Doctor Azgore told me to only take my pill in daylight, and

the sun wasn't up yet, so I was a little more myself than I've been lately. Like Superman, powerless under the wrong sun.

Limo dropped me off at the gate, and Norbert was there waiting for me with a headset and a clipboard. Does he not know about cell phones? It feels like you don't need a headset or a clipboard if you have an Android. Also:

'Norbert, I thought you were the Secret Prince of Netflix. Why are you still working as Douglas' assistant?'

'*Executive* assistant,' he corrected, and he motioned for me to follow him.

I guess relaunching *Regulus* is more interesting than whatever else Secret Princes get up to.

I got a badge and, for some reason, a blindfold. Norbert spun me around three times and then led me by the hand the last part of the way. Which was a weird choice, because as far as I could tell there was only the one building on the lot and it was honking huge and it was right there on the far side of the parking lot.

But maybe the Secret Prince had a Secret Studio he didn't want people to know about?

When he took the blindfold off, I was on the bridge of the Regulus. Or, well, mosta the bridge. They gotta put the cameras somewhere. It was exactly like the original, just not cheap-as-shit. This was built for big-budget Netflix sci-fi 4K Ultra HD. All the buttons and levers and switches placed exactly like the original. Computer displays. Every blinky light. So many blinky lights! The leather seats. Miggsy's flight controls. Nil's science station. Braddock's command chair.

The places where the other two characters stood.

I maybe cried a little. This was like stepping onto the

Enterprise. Into the TARDIS. This was just just

'Pretty cool, huh?'

I turned and Ryan-fucking-Gosling was standing next to me. He was wearing a t-shirt and jeans, which seemed underdressed and also the wrong century for his character.

'You're Ryan Gosling,' I said. I assume people tell him that a lot.

He agreed, and then he said, 'And you're Pat Hinkle, right?'

I nodded slowly and also maybe my mouth was hanging open a little.

Ryan Gosling patted me on the back with Ryan Gosling's hand. 'Sorry about your mom, dude.'

'Yeah,' I muttered. For a split second, I wondered whether Ryan Gosling had killed my mom. Probably not. And I asked, 'You're really doing this? You're doing *Regulus*? You could be doing anything right now.'

He shrugged. 'Secretly, I'm a huge nerd.'

Fair.

Douglas walked over, with Norbert behind him. Norbert gave Ryan a coffee and directed him off somewhere. 'So what do you think?' Douglas asked.

I looked around again. Breathed it in. 'I think the Hyperspace Con is gonna be big this year.'

He flashed a smile. 'Ronkonkoma may need to build a bigger hotel.'

We walked the set together. 'You nailed the bridge,' I told him, 'but what about the rest of the universe? You really gonna shoot this whole thing in New York?'

'We have the AR wall they've been using for *The Mandalorian* and *Star Trek*. And we have a lot of sound stages. We'll do some location shooting at the end. The local tax breaks are nice, but staying in New York was mostly for Nigel. Did you know he hasn't left the city in thirty years?'

I did not know that, but also it sounded extremely true.

He showed off some of his favorite details. In the original series, Nil's computer display was always the same static image: a hand-drawn sine wave. Now, it was a real responsive touchscreen with CG graphics and animated elements. A few of which were…

…inappropriate for a family audience. Fucking Douglas.

I thanked him anyway, for inviting me and for showing me around.

What I really wanted to know was: Why was I there?

'Why are y—?' he sputtered. 'All of this is because of you, Henr—'

'Patr—'

'In the old days, I never fit in with the rest of them. I was always the odd one out. The weirdo. The skulker. When I came back, I thought things were going to be different. I was older, successful. But then I mentioned that I work at Netflix, someone got the wrong idea, and suddenly I was lying to everybody about a reboo—'

'Relaunch.'

'—blaunch. And the attention was nice. Honestly leading those fuckers on a little was nice. But at the end of the day, it just made me feel like a creep again. But you, you got me to admit my shit! I apologized, and these motherfuckers accepted it. Accepted me. And it didn't stop there. You're the one who introduced Norbert to *Regulus*. You're the one who finally got me in the same room as Nigel Kent. All of this, all of this, is happening because of you.

'So anyway,' he said, 'thank you.' And then he motioned for somebody to come over. An older guy, maybe in his eighties? Nineties? Or, okay, maybe that's too old. He was thin, pale, balding. Thick glasses. Three-piece suit. Cane. And, I dunno, just an air of alertness. His eyes were always flicking one way or the other. Taking it all in. And he had a twitch to his lips, like a barely suppressed giggle.

Like he was remembering a very good joke.

Douglas introduced us. 'Henr—'

'Patrick,' I corrected.

'Patrick Henry Hinkle, meet Alfred Norton. Alfie is showrunning.'

Alfie Norton. Of original series genie episode and *Bridgerton* season two fame. We were both at the con last year, but never in the same room. Suddenly all the jokes about how bad the genie episode was seemed mean.

Because Alfie is very, very old.

I guess maybe they were funnier in the past? When he was less old?

He extended his hand, frail and quivering. 'It's a pleasure to meet you, Patrick,' he said. 'Of course, I know all about you.'

I shook his hand delicately. He seemed very breakable.

'I'm so sorry about your mother,' he said.

I changed the subject. 'Set looks great,' I said. 'And I heard Nigel say that he really likes your scripts!'

Alfie nodded. Took me by the shoulder and walked me a few

feet away. I guess so we could talk about something without Douglas? He still wasn't that far away. 'I've been thinking about what I might do next. After all this. And Douglas told me about your journal.'

'He did?'

'Yes, yes.' He grinned, and oh God his teeth were… roughly as bad as mine are.

And he asked me, 'How would you like to be a movie?'

So. Um.

Normally that's where I'd end a chapter, and I woulda here too. Good line to go out on, right? Except for the thing that happened next: My phone rang. Ringer set to a comfortable volume. Detective Bogdonavich calling. Marilyn. I answered.

'Mister Hinkle,' she said.

Alfie was glaring at me. He had just asked me a very cool-sounding question, probably one he'd put alotta thought into, and here I was taking a phone call.

I held up a finger and said, 'Detective. How can I help you?'

'It's the Van Nuys Pants Bandit,' she told me. 'He's struck again. He's in New York.'

FIFTY

Detective Stuart met me at security. With this full-on Victorian handlebar moustache. Amazing.

He flashed his badge, and they let me through a side gate. This was my first time at an airport since the Pandemic. It was noisy and crowded and nobody was wearing a mask.

It was uncomfortable. I was uncomfortable.

Don't get me wrong. I wasn't wearing a mask either. Fuck. When was the last time I even bought an N95? Before Mom died, I guess. But something about being at an airport. All those people. Just made me feel vulnerable. Exposed.

Detective Stuart ushered me up an escalator. Thanked me for coming. Said, 'We could use another set of eyes on this.'

I said, 'You know I'm not actually a detective, right?'

He said, 'You're an amateur detective with a gimmick. Police work with ADWAGs all the time. Matlock was a real guy. It's fine.'

That didn't sound right. Also, 'I have a gimmick?'

'Well, you're very close to the case,' he said, 'and according to your file, you maybe have superpowers now.'

'I…' I stopped. Well, we were on an escalator, so technically I kept going up. 'I have a file that says that?'

Detective Stuart squinted at me for a half-beat, then apologized. 'I misspoke just now,' he said. 'What I meant to say is that you *don't* have a secret file I can't talk about.'

We got off the escalator, rounded a corner. A half-dozen uniformed cops were standing outside a restroom marked off with caution tape. Men's entrance to the left, women's to the right. We ducked under the caution tape, and Detective Stuart led me right.

It smelled like chlorine and death in there. Lights were out, burnt out maybe, except for the ones above each stall. Those were flickering randomly red-to-green-to-red, which combined into this sickly yellow color, because I dunno. Science or whatever.

Victim's outline was taped out on the floor. Well, the outline of her legs. That was as much as I could see, extended out from underneath a stall door. She musta been killed inside.

'How long did it take?' I asked. 'To find her.'

'Too long,' said Detective Stuart. 'This is usually a busy bathroom, but it was late when she died. Airport's supposed to shut down at midnight. They call it a curfew. Something about noise complaints. This isn't normally my beat. Anyway, lady came in on one of the last flights. Staff missed her when they were ushering everybody out, and then there was some scheduling mix-up with the cleaning crews.'

'When did they find her, Stuart?'

'About four hours later.'

'And you're sure it was the Van Nuys Pants Bandit?'

'M.O. checks out. Lethal blunt force trauma to the head. Pants stolen.'

That seemed definitive. 'And what do you think I can do?' I asked.

He shrugged. 'Amateur detective this shit. If I knew what to tell you, we wouldn't need an amateur detective.'

Fair.

I waved my hand under the paper towel dispenser and pulled off a sheet. Used the paper towel to push open the stall door. I immediately regretted that decision. The tape outline carried on up the front of the toilet to the edge of the bowl. There was a splatter of dried blood and cracked porcelain where the head woulda been. Outline suggested that the neck was bent at an… *unnatural* angle. I felt queasy. Couldn't help myself. Threw up into the toilet.

A couple times.

Detective Stuart helped me back up. I apologized. He said it happens. But shit. It hit me worse than when I saw Mom. Something about the pill maybe?

Took a minute. Used the paper towel to wipe vomit from the corner of my mouth. Closed my eyes. 'His flight came in,' I said. 'He stayed behind. Hid till the last passenger from the last flight stopped to use the bathroom. And he killed her. Took her pants.'

'That's our theory.'

I opened my eyes. Took a look at the ceiling. Walked out. Under the tape. Looked across the hall. Down the hall. Through the crowds. Over their heads. There was a restaurant across the way. A bakery. A pretty fancy snack and magazine place.

Is LaGuardia fancy now? Probably not important.

Detective Stuart followed me out.

'There must be cameras all over the place,' I said. He agreed. 'Did they catch anything?'

'Nada. No idea how he got in or out, unless he's got magic powers.'

'Do you—?'

'We don't think he has magic powers.'

My eyes glowed green.

Place was crowded. Hard to know for sure. But I thought maybe I heard somebody calling my name? Looked around. Stupid. Probably some other Pat. Or a Matt. Or just somebody shouting, 'Hat!' real loud 'cause somebody dropped a hat.

Tried to remember if I'd ever actually been to LaGuardia before. With my mom maybe? Woulda been years and years ago. But where would we have gone?

Realized I'd been spaced out for a minute. Detective Stuart was looking at me expectantly. This is it, he was probably thinking. He's doing the thing.

I don't think I was doing a thing, unless the thing was 'forgetting if I'd ever been to LaGuardia.' I don't think they make detective shows about people who can't remember whether they've been to specific airports. Unless? I dunno. There's alotta TV these days.

Thought about the two murders. My mom and this lady. Mom was at home. Killer sought her out. It was personal. He knew her. Broke down a door to get to her. Beat her with her own bat. Shitfucker was angry. But this lady? At the airport? He waited in that bathroom. For hours, he waited. Not for this lady. Just for the opportunity.

'Killer had a motive,' I told Detective Stuart, 'when he killed my mom. But this? No. This he did for fun.'

FIFTY-ONE

'Tell me something about my father.'

Sasha took a long, slow sip from her coffee cup, stared out across the river, and smiled.

This is the story she told me. A true story. More or less.

Lester Jacks was an all-around genius, but he was best at math. Show him some new rule or formula and he'd get it immediately, understand it perfectly. Do all the work in his head preferably. And he'd never get a question wrong. Until he got bored.

He was a solid B+ student.

The teachers always wanted Lester to 'apply himself.' To try harder. To pay attention. To check his work. Lester wanted to rush home to read Tolkien and Jack Kirby comics and listen to prog rock and paint fantasy miniatures and imagine weird worlds. And smoke pot. Lester smoked alotta pot.

And, yes, the folks who didn't know Lester very well assumed the pot was the problem. That it hollowed out his brain. Made him check out. Give up. But the pot came last. The pot was the mellow at the end of Lester's road. When the world was too much noise.

And the world was always too much noise for Lester. Too many rules to follow. Too many voices to listen to. Too many people to disappoint. Nobody more than Lester himself.

Because Lester had dreams. Big dreams. So many dreams. He wanted to play in a rock band. Draw Silver Surfer comics. Write big, chonking fantasy novels about elves and orcs and shit. And he coulda. He knew it. Coulda done any of it. All of it.

If he coulda just 'applied himself.'

Lester first attempted suicide when he was fourteen. It was the night he saw *Star Wars*, and he realized he'd never make anything that beautiful.

He survived, and also he had to buy his parents a new toaster.

After high school, he went to college, because that's what his dad wanted. And after college, he got a job on Wall Street, because that's what his dad wanted. He figured somebody oughta get what they wanted.

And Lester made a shit-ton of money. More money than he knew what to do with. For himself. For other people. For his bosses, most of all. 'You can write your own ticket,' they said.

'Where to?' he asked.

'Anywhere,' they said.

But as Lester looked out his penthouse window, into the night and the lights of the city, all he saw were the numbers. Interest rates. Exchange rates. Margins. And when he slept, he dreamt of math. Of unsolvable equations. Of variables that flickered and swam.

And never a single elf.

One day he bought a sandwich from a street vendor and walked down to Battery Park. Sat in the grass and watched the ferries. And he thought about how he was gonna kill himself. Maybe jump off the roof of his apartment building. He had roof access.

He'd really hafta hoof it to clear the awnings.

He smiled to himself as he pulled the pickles that he hadn't ordered off the sandwich that he had. Set them on the paper bag he'd flattened out in front of him.

'Y'know…' somebody said. A woman. Standing over him. In a floral dress. Pair of Doc Martens. Denim jacket. Couple homemade buttons.

One said 'I WISH FOR ONE LESS GENIE.'

This woman was a few years younger than Lester maybe. Short. A little plain. A sheaf of papers in one hand.

She half-blocked the sun.

Lester squinted up at her. In his suit and tie. His grass-stained butt. A little mayo on his fingers maybe. 'Do I know what?'

'Ben Franklin,' she said, 'said, "Hunger is the best pickle."'

Lester wasn't sure why he was having this conversation, but he theorized, 'Because Franklin would've rather starved to death than eat a pickle?'

She crouched down to look him in the eye. 'Because people put pickles on things to make them taste better.' She looked at Lester's pickles. 'Some people. Specific people. But nothing makes food taste better than being hungry for it.'

Lester looked down at his pickles. Then at her, crouched in

front of him. 'Are you… selling me something?' he asked.

'What are you hungry for?' she asked him.

Lester hesitated. Tried to remember. To imagine. A lonely alien surfing ancient suns. A hobbit placing his first furry foot onto foreign lands. An endless sky, full of light and color and the most beautiful music.

Weird worlds, somehow less weird than this one.

'Here,' she said. And she handed him a flyer. A xerox of a xerox of a xerox maybe. Hand-typed, with a crudely-drawn starship streaking past Saturn.

He looked at it. Then back at her. Set down his sandwich. Then back to the flyer.

'What is this?' he asked.

She smiled. 'There's a TV show,' she said, 'that I think you're gonna wanna see.'

FIFTY-TWO

'Is there anything I should know about Alfie Norton?' I asked
Marv over the phone as I tried to tie my tie for the third or fourth
time. It kept coming out too long or too short and also weirdly
hung to one side. I can't remember the last time I wore a tie, but
I remember not being able to tie it then either.

It's the sorta thing that I'd ask Lilly for help with, but she was
at work already.

'He thinks he's funnier than he is,' said Marv.

'Who?' I asked.

'Did you take your pill yet today?' he asked. People who
know have started asking me that. A lot. Like, now that they
know I'm on medication, anything I do or say that's weird, that
doesn't meet their expectations, that they don't like, it must be
because I didn't take my pill.

There was a moment when I first considered whether I had
ADHD when I thought maybe it was okay. To be me. After

twenty-seven years on this Earth. With all my… *quirks*. If I had ADHD, it meant that my brain worked differently. That I was 'neurodivergent.' Which wasn't a good thing or a bad thing. Just different.

But I was wrong. Different is wrong. Officially, medically-certified wrong. If there's a pill? That means it's an illness to be cured. And if you don't take that cure? When it's right there in front of you? What does that make you? Lazy? Weak? Wrong?

So there's that disappointment in their tone. That judgment. And that sense of shame I feel. But also an anger, yeah? Like, we disagree about something because I'm wrong? I'm wrong? Maybe you're the one who needs a fucking pill. Maybe what I said or thought or did was fine. Maybe I was right. Maybe it had nothing to do with whether I took a fucking pill, you motherfucker-shit-fuckshitter.

Maybe. Maybe.

'No, Marv.' I kinda snapped at him. Winced. Wondered whether I should let him off the hook. 'No, I haven't taken my pill today.'

Had to let him off the hook.

'Y'know, I have ADHD,' I said, 'so sometimes I forget to do things like…' I said the joke. Everything's okay again, if you say the joke. '…like cure my ADHD.'

Marv didn't say anything, but then I laughed, so he could laugh. He did.

'Maybe take your pill before your meeting?' he suggested.

I grabbed an earring box off my dresser and opened it. Green light spilled out into the room. I pulled out the pill and popped it into my mouth. Swallowed. Eyes felt warm.

'Anything else?' I asked.

'Yeah,' said Marv. 'Don't mention the genie episode. Alfie is still sore about that one. He really liked that episode.'

I cringed. 'Really?' I said. 'But it's sooo bad. Should I even be working with this guy?'

'Other things he's written have been better. Have you watched *Bridgerton* season two yet?'

I had not. Pill was kicking in. Sighed. Tied my tie. Straight. Correct length. Pulled on my suit jacket. 'So just to clarify,' I said, 'I should ask him lots of questions about the genie episode and specifically why it's so awful?'

'And there's the pill,' said Marv. 'Good luck!'

I didn't need luck though. I had science.

I was seven minutes early to the restaurant. In Midtown. French. According to Google Translate, the name of the restaurant was 'The Good Soup.' Because I guess it's hard to get a table at 'The Great Soup' midday on a Tuesday?

Alfie arrived with Douglas and Norbert. For some reason, I thought it was just gonna be the two of us. Probably because Alfie said, and I quote: 'It'll just be the two of us.' I remember stuff much better when I've taken my pill.

We said hello, shook hands. Douglas apologized, but said when he heard about the project, he wanted in. Norbert said Douglas still had one more wish left, so I should humor him.

We sat. And ordered soup. In French. I mean, probably I ordered soup. I don't speak French. When I pointed to the menu and asked, 'Is this soup?' everybody just laughed. I mean, who knows? Maybe I'd ordered 'gratuity included.'

Alfie said something to the waiter in French and the waiter

smiled and nodded and left us alone for a while. Alfie set his briefcase on the table. Pulled out a copy of my journal. This journal that I'm writing in right now. A scan. Of everything through the end of part two, as it would turn out. In a manilla file folder. He flipped it open to show me.

'How did you—?' I began, but he shook his head.

'The source is unimportant.' Unimportant? It was important to me! I thought through all the people who had read my journal by then: Marv. Lilly. Sasha. Douglas and Norbert. The most likely suspects. Nigel twice. He'd forgotten he'd read it, and I didn't have the heart to tell him. Lydia, and I hope she's forgiven me. Nihal from the bodega. I dunno. He was interested. Okay. Shit. Alotta people have read my journal.

'What matters,' said Alfie, 'is that I read it. And I loved it!'

'Loved it?' I repeated. That didn't sound right.

'Yes,' he said. 'The pathos. The humor.'

I tried to correct him. 'It's about my dead mom. It's not supposed to be funny.'

He frowned. 'I see it as a comedy with a few isolated moments of pathos.'

Just then, a series of extremely serious things happened. Somebody was shot dead. Another person had to put their cat to sleep. A third person, I dunno, discovered a new vaccine that'll save millions and millions of lives or whatever. Stuff like that.

Not in the French soup restaurant, obviously, but somewhere near there probably.

My point is that this journal is very serious.

'I didn't understand the ending,' Alfie confessed. 'Is there more? Are you still writing?'

I was. You may have noticed. And I said so.

'And you're still planning to catch your dear mother's killer?' he asked. 'How do you intend to do that?'

I wasn't sure if I should say. What the detectives told me. What I'd seen at LaGuardia. Maybe just the broad strokes. 'The cops still think it mighta been the Van Nuys Pants Bandit,' I said. 'Turns out he's still on the loo—'

'Trouser Bandit,' said Alfie.

'Excuse me?'

'Where I come from,' he explained, 'pants are underwear. But the Van Nuys serial killer steals outerwear. He steals trousers. *Trouser* Bandit is more precise.' He flipped through my journal until he found a page with the words 'Pants Bandit' written out. Tapped the words. Took a red pen from his inside pocket, uncapped it with his crooked old British teeth, crossed out the word 'Pants,' and scrawled 'Trousers' overtop. Spat the pen cap into his hand. 'You see? If we want to attract an international audience for our movie?' He turned the page to face me. Pocketed the pen. '*Trousers.*'

I took the page. Looked at the red ink over my handwriting. My words. Set it down.

'I dunno if this is a good idea,' I said, maybe feeling a little faint.

I could see Douglas and Norbert were disappointed. Alfie was… not ready to take no for an answer. 'Your story will always exist as your story,' he explained. 'For you. But a movie is for everyone! It takes hundreds of people to make a movie. And millions will see it! Do you want that? Or do you want your "pants"?'

I shook my head. It didn't feel right. My mom's dead. The killer's still out there.

'I think we can get you six figures for the rights.'

I started to say something. I'm not sure what. Like, I dunno, 'It's not about the money.' Or, 'I can't sell my life.' Or, 'Your genie story was ass.'

But the waiter brought our soups.

Alfie scowled at him as he shuffled his papers back into his suitcase and off the table.

'You'll think about it,' said Alfie. To me. Not as a question. Like a command, I guess.

I looked down at my soup. Poked at it. Was there an octopus in there?

Alfie had turned to Douglas, started talking to him. Normally I'd be too distracted by the that-can't-really-be-an-octopus-can-it? that I wouldn'ta heard them. But the pill.

'I've been meaning to come here for a while,' said Douglas.

Alfie agreed. 'Absolutely,' he said. 'Four stars.'

Four stars.

'Did you know,' Lilly asked me once, 'that Regulus is actually four stars?'

I didn't. Or I did, and I'd forgotten.

'Sometimes you think it's just one thing,' she told me, right before we had sex, 'and it turns out to be a whole bunch of different, more complicated things.'

One.

Who was your dad? His name was Lester Jacks.

Two.

What's wrong with you? I have pretty bad ADHD.

Three.

Why did Mom walk away from *Regulus*? Marv threatened her.

Four.

Who killed her?

I looked across the table. Alfie and Douglas were laughing hard over some joke I'd missed. Too hard. Douglas was humoring Alfie, I was sure. He knows the thing Marv told me earlier: 'He thinks he's funnier than he is.' He was being a good exec, humoring the talent.

But Alfie? That laugh? So weird. Arhythmic. Like what aliens think human laughter sounds like. None of it real. He was wearing a mask. Like me. To hide his true self. To walk among them. But it wasn't ADHD. It was something else. It was

  was

   was

'*Trouser bandit*,' I whispered.

My eyes flashed green.

FIFTY-THREE

They put me through to Detective Marilyn Bogdonavich.

'I think I found him,' I said with a trembling, too eager voice. Then I corrected myself: 'I-I know I found him.'

'You think or you know,' she shot back to me. 'Which is it?'

'Um.' I paused to think. Maybe I shoulda asked for Detective Stuart. Maybe he's Good Cop. 'The first one, I guess. If I'm being literal. But definitely also the second one too, if I'm, being, uh…'

'If you're being what? Metaphorical? You know metaphorically who killed your mother?'

That didn't sound right. I struggled to say something sensible. To put syllables together into words. Failing that, I just made this weird noise at her. Pounded the heel of my palm against my temple. Tried again. 'It's Alfie-fucking-Norton.'

'Who?'

'He…' I hesitated to explain. To sound any crazier than I already did. Shit. Had I taken my medication today? Fuck. Was

I pulling that 'Did you take your medication?' bullshit on myself now?

'He's not another one of your *Regulus* pals, is he?' she asked. She didn't wait for me to answer. 'Y'know, I found one of those episodes at a garage sale last month? On a VHS! It was all *Magnum PI*s and then this one cheap-ass sci-fi show at the end. I told my wife, "This shit better not be what I think it is!" But then it was! And I don't know, Pat. It's not as bad as I thought it'd be! I mean, it was bad. Real, real bad. More spells and shit than I thought there'd be. But it definitely could've been worse. Shit. I would've rather it was a little worse! Wasn't fun making fun of it. Just sa—'

I hung up on her. I needed proof. Evidence. I needed somebody to hack his files. Like in the movies.

Or in books, probably? Probably I should read more.

Who did I know who was good with computers? Lilly, maybe? No. She keeps getting us locked out of our ConEd account because she can't remember our password. Marv? No. He still has a Yahoo! email address.

Lydia. Lydia used to work for a security company. Chapter thirty-six. Facts!

I'd done some horrible things to her. Lied. Snuck around her apartment. Lied about sneaking around her apartment. But she'd read my journal, read everything in context. She musta forgiven me, right?

'I haven't completely forgiven you,' she said as she opened up her apartment door. 'But we all loved your mother, so I guess I'll give you one more chance.' She gave me a hug. She smelled like my mom. She invited me in.

I sat on her couch and drank her tea while I explained everything to her. The Van Nuys Pants Bandit. The Van Nuys *Trouser* Bandit. Alfie Norton.

The thing I forgot, even with my pill, is that Lydia was the one who invited Alfie to Hyperspace Con every year. They were friends. Or. Well. Friendly, I guess. She'd known Alfie for years, and she didn't think he was capable of murder.

'You don't think he's a little off?' I asked.

She chuckled. 'Honey,' she said, and she put a hand on my shoulder. 'We're all a little off. Marv and Eileen are on the spectrum. Douglas gets panic attacks. Nigel has early onset dementia. Becky's bipolar. I have PTSD. You have ADHD. Your mom had whatever she had. That's why we found each other.' Looked me in the eye. 'Why we forgive each other.'

'Forgive…' The tea was really good. Warm. Smoky. If Alfie and Lydia were secretly in cahoots, this is where she woulda poisoned me to death. I'm not dead. But I asked anyway. Kinda. Technically all I said was 'Cahoots?'

'What now?' she asked. She got up to take her own cup to the kitchen.

'I really think it's him,' I called after her. 'Are you really, really sure it's not?'

She set her cup down on the counter. Stopped. Got quiet for a minute. 'Really, *really* sure?' she asked. And she looked at me like she wasn't.

One interesting fact about Lydia is that she's an amazingly fast typist. I hunt and peck. I'm always looking at the keyboard. Forget what word I'm on. Hafta look back at the screen. There's a reason I'm writing all of this longhand. But Lydia?

It was like watching somebody play a piano. Play a symphony.

First, she was in his hospital records. Found his birth certificate. And I was not wrong. Alfred Newton was old as shit. Born in 1928. Turning ninety-five. Father, Geoffrey. Deceased. Died 1943. That wasn't on his birth certificate. She'd moved on. Mother, Estelle *not* deceased. Holy Hell. One hundred and twelve. And still living in England. Town called Bog's Bottom. Sounded made-up.

Lydia pointed out that all names were made-up at some point.

It's all made-up.

Alfred has two current addresses. One in England. But not in Bog's Bottom. In London. I've heard of London. And one in Los Angeles. Sherman Oaks. I made Lydia pull up Google Maps. Probably I coulda done that part. Sherman Oaks was right below Van Nuys on the screen. An eleven-minute drive, dot to dot.

'Zoom in,' I said. 'Do street view.'

And now I was staring at his apartment building. White. Terraced. Which was his window? If she zoomed in far enough, could we see him?

My eyes felt warm. 'His credit card statements,' I said. 'Can you get his credit card statements?' She could. She found plane tickets. 'Can you get into his flight info?'

He took the red eye into LaGuardia the same day that woman was killed. The morning of. He didn't check into his hotel until the next day. The day we met.

'February,' I whispered. 'Last year.'

He was in New York the day my mom died.

Lydia pulled her hands back from the keyboard. Made a sound like a gasp into a whimper. Began to cry. To sob. With her whole body. In heaves.

Not me. I had no tears left. My eyes were hot. Like fire. And the room… The room was green.

And I could hear her.

My mom.

Singing.

I've been thinking a lot about Regulus.

And I whispered, 'I'm gonna kill the shit out of Alfie Norton.'

FIFTY-FOUR

'Welcome to Hyperspace Hype, the official unofficial official podcast for *Regulus*, the once and future sci-fi classic! I'm Marvin Casiano.'

'And I'm "THE" Becky Stratton.'

Marv and Becky recorded their podcast over Zoom. I was in my apartment, cross-legged on my couch, no pants, with a pair of headphones on. Marv and Becky were inside little squares on my screen. Not literally. Marv was recording from his apartment. Becky was back in England for a while.

Marv plugged their sponsor. 'Hyperspace Hype is brought to you by Mark's Comics. Visit any of their three New York locations or order online and get your comics shipped straight to your door. Now serving forty-eight states and for-some-reason Staten Island. No matter how you shop, Mark's Comics are your comics!'

And Becky added a perfunctory, 'Get 10% off of your first

purchase with promo code Hype2023.'

After that they did some banter. Marv talked about almost buying a cat. Becky talked about wrapping up her UK tour. 'I've been back long enough,' she said, 'that I'm starting to remember why I left.'

'So why did you leave?' Marv asked.

'Everything. All of it.'

'You forgot "all of it"?'

She shrugged in her little square. 'It's a lot to remember.'

Then Marv introduced me. 'First up, we're joined by Pat Hinkle. Pat is a second-generation *Regulus* fan with a hilarious story about how he discovered the show.'

I squinted at Marv in his little square. 'The fuck, Marv?'

He frowned. 'We can cut that out. Just tell them a story about how you discovered *Regulus* that doesn't involve your mom being murdered or me forcing her out of the community twenty-five years ago because she called me the f-word.'

I forced a smile. 'Well, I was at a garage sale, Marv, and I found a VHS tape that was all *Magnum P.I.*s with one *Regulus* at the end.'

'For our younger listeners,' Becky interjected, 'vee-haitch-ess stands for "Vintage Hipster Shit."'

Things went smoother from there. I talked about my favorite episodes: The first one. The time loop episode. The time loop episode. And about visiting the set of the relaunch. I said nice things about the set.

'And speaking of the relaunch,' said Becky, 'let's bring on our second guest, showrunner for the new series: Alfred Norton!'

I did not know this was about to happen. Two squares

became three, as Alfie-fucking-Norton's fucking face appeared on my fucking screen. With that terrifying, twitchy lip.

'Lovely to see you all,' he said. 'And you Patrick! Yes, yes, able young man.'

I mumbled something incoherent back, I think. Like, 'You too are able also.' Even with the pill, that moment's a panicked blur.

'I'm sure everybody's excited to hear about the new show,' said Marv, either not noticing or not acknowledging my disorientation, 'but let's start with your work on the original series. You came to the show rather late, yeah?'

'Oh yes oh yes,' said Alfie. 'I'd been writing for the BBC for years at that point, on various drama series, literary adaptations and such, but I'd never done science-fiction. I knew the script editor for *Regulus* a little though, just from around the canteen, chap named Biff Langley, and he asked me to write a script for the second seas—'

Marv tried to get a word in. 'You wrote "Bonfires Bey—"'

'"Bonfires Beyond Your Fondest Horizon,' yes. And everyone was quite pleased with that one. Isn't that right, Becks?'

Becky had been on mute. Took herself off. 'One of my favorites, Alf. Good Miggs episode. Cheers for that.' Back on mute.

'After that,' he continued, 'they asked me to do another and another. I wrote four episodes all toge—'

I'd just about regained my wits. Jumped in. 'Including the genie episode, right?' I said it like a question, but obviously we all knew he wrote it. Anybody who's ever seen the old show probably knows it. I'm a comparative newcomer to *Regulus* fandom, compared to Marv and the rest, but if I know one thing about the fans, I know this:

Everybody hates the genie episode.

Alfie scrunched his face into a disapproving glare-frown. Marv had told me the other day, in a different context, not to bring up that episode. That Alfie hates talking about that episode. And I'd followed his advice then. But that's when I was trying to get on Alfie's good side.

Before I realized that Alfie Norton doesn't have a good side.

'That was kinda a weird one, huh?' I needled.

He stammered. Muttered. Swore maybe, low enough that the mics didn't catch it.

'Pat!' Marv scolded. Then he apologized to Alfie. 'We can edit this part out, Alfie.'

I wasn't done though. 'Too bad we can't edit out the whole genie episode, amirite?'

Marv shouted my name again, but Alfie shook his head. Raised a hand. He'd collected himself. 'No no no. It's quite all right, Marvin. I know that particular episode has a bit of a… reputation in the community.'

'Does it?' I asked innocently. 'I didn't know.'

Marv tried to change the subject. 'Maybe we can go back to "Bonf—"'

But I'd gotten to Alfie. 'Biff felt that the second season had gotten quite dreary by the end,' he explained. 'He asked me to write something lighter. Something with some jokes in it. Roland and Becks were both comedians, after all. And I'd always wanted to try my hand at panto. Who doesn't love a goofy genie? It was great fun.'

Marv's moustache trembled. I knew how Marv felt about that episode. He was trying so hard to keep his cool. I kinda wanted him to lose it.

'And was it?' I asked Alfie. 'Was it *great fun?*'

'You have to understand,' said Alfie, 'that in the UK, *Regulus* was considered a family show. A show for children. It's only when it came to America that it was embraced by… young adults. Before it was taken so…'

The corners of Alfie's lips curled into a quivering smile.

'…seriously.'

'WHY IS THERE A GENIE IN OUTER SPACE?' Marv shouted. Accidentally spit a little. Surprised himself. Was immediately embarrassed. Immediately regretted it. Cupped his face in one hand.

'Oh, Marvin,' said Alfie, in sing-song condescension, 'you of *allll* people…'

'He's saying that because you're gay,' I clarified. Because I wanted to make it worse. 'And because he's a crochety old man.'

Marv looked up. Scowled through a clenched jaw. At me. At Alfie. Eyed Becky, and she took herself off mute.

'I think that episode get a bad rap,' she said. 'I quite liked the musical number. And the livestock they brought in, mostly.'

Alfie chuckled. 'Yes, thank you. Though I'm not sure that Roland appreciated me turning his character into a horse for half the episode.'

'Did you retire after that?' I asked. 'Because that's your last credit on IMDB for alm—'

Alfie's eyes narrowed. His mouth straightened. 'I did not retire,' he snapped. 'I pursued other work.'

I laughed. 'Too bad you never caught any!'

Becky laughed too. Almost muted in time.

Alfie snarled, stood, and suddenly we were looking at his crotch.

'Look!' I pointed at his little box on my screen. 'Crochety!'

Becky was cry-laughing on mute. Marv was just frowning and shaking his head.

Alfie's box cut to black, then disappeared.

'The fuck, Pat?' Marv snarled.

I took a slow, deep breath. Leaned in towards my camera. Any hint of a smile was gone from my face.

I said, 'Here's the thing, guys. I'm pretty sure Alfie Norton killed my mom.'

FIFTY-FIVE

I got Becky's email when I turned off airplane mode at LAX. Her report from Bog's Bottom:

Alfie Norton was with Douglas and Norbert and Nigel and Gosling and the rest of them in New York. Busy with filming. Perfect time for me to slip away. Investigate.

The Van Nuys Pants Bandit had killed twice in New York, if you count my mother, which I very much did at this point, but sixteen times in Van Nuys. There had to be some clue out here. Some physical evidence.

Took an Uber to his condo. It looked just like on Google Street View. White stucco walls. Black terraces. Flanked by palm trees. Found the buzzer for Norton. Buzzed his neighbor. Who buzzed me in without me even needing to do a bit with a silly accent.

Californians are rubes.

Climbed the stairs to Alfie's apartment. Knocked. Just in case he had, like, a dog sitter or whatever. No answer. Tried the door. Just in case he… I dunno, had a dog sitter who forgot to lock his door. Anyway, it was locked.

I knocked on the neighbor's door. The one who buzzed me in without asking any questions. The rube.

Guy answered the door. Grumbly. Messy hair. Hadn't shaved. T-shirt had holes in it. Still in his boxers and apparently fine with that. I get it. Life's a lot.

He glared at me. Like I was interrupting him.

'Sorry to interrupt you,' I said. Mostly it was the pill talking, I think.

'Too late for that,' he said. 'Whaddaya want?'

He sounded like a New Yorker. Came out here to... what? Busy in his apartment in the middle of the day. Saw his laptop out on the coffee table. Maybe just a work-from-home guy like me, but I took a chance.

'Are you a screenwriter?' I asked. He glared. 'Did you know your neighbor Alfred is a screenwriter?'

'The old guy?'

'Yeah. He wrote for *Bridgerton*.'

'Season one?'

'No.'

He made a little grunt noise like that was the wrong answer.

'Anyway, he's in New York,' I continued. 'They're shooting a new show. And here I am in LA, and he asks me to grab some notes from his apartment, but I left the key he left me... somewhere. Not important.'

It was a really great lie, I thought, and if he didn't believe me, it was his fault.

I don't think he believed me.

'Anyway, I was wondering if I could dangle from your terrace and climb over onto his terrace, so I can break into his apartment?'

He didn't have an immediate answer to that, except he was staring at me like I was a lunatic. Which was not *not* an answer.

'Look,' I said, 'I know this is a big ask. Do me a solid, and I'll put you in touch with one of the producers on Alfie's show. They're gonna need another writer soon.' Because Alfie was gonna be in jail or dead.

'On *Bridgerton* season three?' he asked.

'Yeah, no. The new thing. It's a space show.'

Nerds love space. And everybody's a nerd these days. His eyes lit up. But I could tell he was still skeptical, because he took a breath and he told me, 'I'm still skeptical.'

I took out my phone and called Douglas-who-keeps-saying-he-owes-me-everything.

Everything in Estelle's kitchen had expired except the tea. So I accepted the tea. She offered me a biscuit from a tin that didn't look like it'd been opened since Thatcher. I thanked her for the tea. She asked me how Alfie was doing. I told her that he was still writing for television.

'There's still television?' she asked.

I asked her some questions about Alfie. About what he was like growing up. But that was ninety years ago. She couldn't remember much. She remembered that Alfie liked to play ball with the other children in the village. She remembered that Alfie and his father didn't get along.

I was perched on the screenwriter's terrace railing, one hand steadying me against the side wall that separated his terrace from Alfie's. Slowly, I stood. So stupid. In my head I thought, Please let my superpower be wall-crawling.

The screenwriter was behind me, by the terrace door, arms folded. 'If you die,' he complained, 'you know they won't gimme that job.'

I glanced back at him. 'It's fine,' I said. 'I've done this before.' Chapter thirty-six.

I'd meant that to be reassuring. He didn't seem reassured.

Decided not to mention that I fell last time.

I pivoted towards the wall. Placed one foot in front of the other. Took a step forward, then another, till I was nose-close to the wall. Lifted my back foot out over the side. Stretched my arm around and gripped the far side with the tips of my fingers. Squooshed the side of my face against the stucco. Swung my dangling foot towards Alfie's terrace railing. Couldn't quite reach.

'Okay,' I said squooshidly. 'If you really wanna be a professional screenwriter, you're gonna hafta come over here and hold my hand.'

She found a dusty old album at the back of one of her cupboards, behind some pickles. The photographs in it were from the 1930s and '40s. Posed black and whites of her and Alfie and her late husband, Geoffrey. He was a big chap with a sour expression. 'What did he do?' I asked. I meant what did her husband do for a living. But she tapped a picture of young Alfie with her fingernail and said, 'He didn't mean to. He was trying to protect me.'

I won't describe the most embarrassing parts, but suffice it to say that the screenwriter held on and I managed to scramble over to Alfie's terrace. I climbed down off his railing, only lightly scratched and bruised.

Alfie's terrace door was locked. Because of course it was. Who knows who might scramble over from the neighbor's terrace? I considered my option. Singular. Alfie's terrace furniture consisted of a lounge chair and a small table to set a drink or a book on. I picked up the table and threw it through the glass door.

I wondered if the screenwriter was gonna call the cops on me.

I wondered if any of the cops would want a job on *Regulus*.

I walked into Alfie's apartment.

(I've tried to capture the dialogue like you do.)

'My Geoffrey was a tailor,' she said, 'with very specific ideas. He used to hit me when I was disrespectful. Or when I disrespected myself.'

'How do you mean?' I asked.

'He felt women were best seen and not heard. That they should obey their husbands no matter what. Dress a certain way. It was a long time ago.'

'Dress a certain way?'

'He was a tailor. Clothes were his vocation. He got quite upset when women wore trousers.'

Except for one overturned table and all that broken glass on the carpet, Alfie's apartment was very tidy. Tidy like Marv's apartment was tidy, which is to say basically empty. Nothing on the walls but the television. One couch, opposite. A writing desk in the corner. Dresser and bed in the bedroom. A few suits in the closet. And that was it.

Marv threw things away to control the chaos. This wasn't that. Alfie wasn't fighting against the chaos. He was hiding it away. I was sure of it.

I checked his drawers. The closet. Checked the couch and the bed. Nothing. Shit.

I sat down on the edge of his bed. Closed my eyes. Remembered.

Chapter eleven. The dark spot left on my mom's rug. Like a hole in the universe. And a thing climbing out of it. A hunch.

I got up. Went to the kitchen. Grabbed the hammer from the tool drawer. Walked back into the living room. Shoved the couch to one side. Rolled up the carpet and pulled up the floorboards, one at a time.

She told me the story of how her husband died. He'd come home early and drunk. She was trying on a pair of trousers her sister had bought her. He was furious. Alfie was playing outside. Came running when he heard her screams.

Alfie Norton beat his father to death with a croquet mallet.

And there it was. Under the floor boards. A croquet mallet. No. 'THE' croquet mallet. From Becky's email. From all those decades ago. And stained with so much blood. Just lacquered with it.

Not from one victim. Or twenty.

Then Alfie turned to his mother, and he spat in her face. He blamed her for provoking his dad. He blamed her for making Alfie kill him.

That was the last time Estelle Norton saw her son. The year was 1943.

Eighty years of murder.

Mom was killed with Roland Yates' cricket bat. He took it from her. Beat her to death with it. But the others.

I'm not sure how long I sat there on the floor of Alfie Norton's apartment, his bloody mallet set across my lap. The sun set. My phone rang. At a reasonable volume. It was Detective Stuart.

'Where are you?' he asked.

'It's not important,' I said.

'We found them, Pat.'

'Found what?' I asked.

'We found the pants.'

FIFTY-SIX

The motherfucking cops believed me. Detective Stuart. Even Detective Bogdonavich. They fucking believed me.

When I called Bogdonavich? When I fingered Norton in chapter fifty-three? They looked into it. Maybe gathered some more evidence, I dunno. Got a warrant. Searched Alfie's hotel room while he was at the studio. Got the manager to open the little black safe. And found a half-dozen pairs of women's pants crumpled and crammed inside. Dried blood on all of them. DNA tests would take a while, but we had him.

We had him.

Also, we lost him. They lost him. Stuart. Bogdonavich. They sent half the NYPD, not literally probably, to the studio to arrest Alfie. Nobody could find him. He'd gone out for a smoke break. Never came back. Did he know? He knew. How did he know?

I got back on the red eye, first flight into LaGuardia. Detective Stuart met me at the gate. I gave him the mallet. 'I don't wanna get your hopes up,' he said, 'but we think your mother's pants were in the wad.'

'Don't call it that,' I said. And I went home and I cried and I slept.

Phone rang at two. Not sure what day. I answered it reflexively.

'Who's this?' I mumbled.

There was no answer. Just silence. For ten seconds. Twenty. Thirty. Then the sounds of an orchestra, tuning their instruments. The call disconnected. Caller unknown.

I stood. Scratched the gunk from my eyes. Shuffled to my dresser. Grabbed a pair of socks. Grabbed an earring box.

Took the pill. Straightened.

Called an Uber. Had to get to Nigel's show. To *Aladdin*.

I ran the last twelve blocks, barreling through crowds of tourists, past street nut vendors and men dressed as cartoon characters. I may have trampled a Pikachu. Stumbled into the lobby of the New Amsterdam just as the first act was letting out. Fell to the floor. Smelly. Fuck, Broadway. Febreeze that shit.

An usher helped me up.

'Nigel,' I said, between pants. 'I need to see Nigel.'

Usher was a good guy. Frank. He helped me down to Nigel's dressing room. He was half out of his parrot costume when I got there. Looked up at me, suddenly worried.

He asked, 'Did I forget something, Patty?'

I shook my head. I was still out in the hall. Another one of the actors knocked into me. Tall. Cut. Goatee. Blue. You can guess which part he was playing.

Wearing nothing but his boxers.

Nigel asked, 'Are you all right?' To him, not me.

Blue guy swore. 'I gotta be on stage in five minutes,' he said, almost cried, 'and some shit stole my genie pants!'

'No,' I corrected him. 'Some shit stole your genie *trousers*.'

FIFTY-SEVEN

I left them. Had to find Alfie. What was he doing here? Why did he take the genie's pants?

Turned a corner and the hall was green. My eyes were green. The hall was green.

My mom was there.

'Mom?' I said. Unsure. Unsure where reality began and ended.

She looked like I remember her. How I always wanna remember her. Young. Beautiful.

Sane.

I pulled her into my arms and hugged her. Tried to ask her questions through my sobs. What are you doing here? How are you here? But my words were incoherent.

She held me. Shushed me. 'It'll be okay,' she said. 'You're almost done.'

But I wasn't listening. 'He's here,' I told her. 'The man who killed you.'

She didn't care about that. She pushed me to arm's length. Looked me in the eye. 'I wanna know about you,' she said. 'I wanna to make sure you're okay.'

I kinda bobbled my head. Not a nod, not a shake. 'I'm trying,' I said. 'Trying to figure things out.' She ran a hand down my arm. 'I know about Dad,' I told her. 'I figured it out. I have ADHD like him. There's a pill I'm taking.'

'I can see that,' she said. Made a face. 'You look… radioactive?'

I shrugged. 'Maybe. I dunno. It's helping. Maybe. With my head. With the writing.'

'And Lilly?'

I wiped tears from my face. 'She's good, Mom. You shoulda met her. She she she woulda liked you. She doesn't give up on people.'

'And your job?'

I was having trouble, in that moment, remembering what I even do for a living. 'I have friends,' I said instead. 'Your friends. Marv and Lydia and Nigel and even Douglas isn't so bad. I found them because of you. I'm so sorry that I never knew you. That I didn't know you till you were gone.'

She touched my face. 'That's not your job, Patty. That was never your job. To know me? Your job was to grow up and get out there. To live your life. I didn't work all those jobs all those years so you could know me. Didn't scrape and save and push myself… Grind myself down…'

Now she was crying too. I took her into my arms again. 'It's okay,' I said. 'You get to rest now.' I could feel her nodding against my chest.

In a halting, sing-song voice, she sang, 'I've been thinking a lot about Regulus…'

'And Marv,' I whispered. Remembered. 'Marv forgives you.'

I could feel her starting to fade.

The very first words I wrote in this journal. 'I will find you.' All this time, I thought I was looking for her killer.

There was so much I still wanted to tell her. To ask her about. To apologize for. For not appreciating her when she was alive. For disappearing from her life when she needed me most. For hiding under a blanket when I was seven years old.

Chapter seven.

I thought she gave up on life. All those years ago. But she didn't. Didn't give up. She chose me. Chose my life. And she never told me I was weird. Never told me I was wrong for being who I was. Never took away Marv's comics, even thought they were deeply, deeply inappropriate for a kid my age.

Chapter two.

When I was little, I had a nightlight. Chapter seventeen. And when you wound it up, it'd play 'Twinkle Twinkle Little Star.' And every night, Mom would sing me to sleep to that song. Over and over, till the nightlight wound down.

And if I wasn't asleep, she'd stop anyway. Wherever the nightlight stopped. Sometimes mid-word. And she'd shrug, and she'd say, 'Sorry, Patty. That's all you get.'

That's all you get.

'Before you go,' I blurted out, 'this this pill I'm taking. The doctor said it might gimme a superpower. All this time, I've been trying to figure out what it is. What my superpower is.'

She looked up at me. She twinkled like starlight.
'It's you, Mom. You've always been my superpower.'
Then she was gone.

FIFTY-EIGHT

The lights flashed, and a voice blared through the theater's speaker system: 'Ladies and gentlemen, take your seats. The second act is about to begin!' It was Alfie Norton's voice, reverberating from every direction. I could hear that piece of shit's smirk.

I dialed Detective Bogdonavich, then tossed my phone to a passing stagehand. Shouted, 'Tell them Alfie Norton is at the show! Tell them Alfie Norton's here.'

And I ran back to Nigel's dressing room.

Elsewhere, a scrawny blue man, bare-chested, in ill-fitted genie trousers took the stage of the New Amsterdam Theater, dragging an over-sized duffle bag behind him, stuffed full of what we would later find out were military-grade explosives. There were murmurs from the audience. Panicked stares from the orchestra.

The blue man laughed along to a joke that only he'd heard.

'I've wired this entire theater with explosives!' he shouted. He was miked up, his voice still coming out of every speaker in the building. 'So you little pissants better do exactly what I say! Alfie Norton makes the wishes now!' There were gasps and screams. A woman fainted probably. 'Audience: keep your seats! Orchestra: it's time for my big number. Hit it!'

He grinned. Winked at the conductor. 'You know which one.'

And so, however reluctantly, the band played.

The genie's big number. *Friend Like Me*. Sort of.

Alfie Norton sang, 'Well, Roland Yates, he had *The Yates Pages*. There was *The Nil Set* for Nigel Kent! But here's the tale,
     where
        I prevail,
It's time for the main *evennnt!*

There's a genius in your presence now,
So much better than a Broadway cast!
And explosives at every exit point,
You know, this matinee could be a blaaast!

His eyes darted side-to-side. He was scanning the audience for me. Scanning the wings.

And I'll say:
'Mister Hinkle, sir,
We'll have so much fun!'
Why don't you find a seat,
While I confess,

I'm not sorry that I killed your mum!
Ha-ha!

Actions have consequence,
It's the same old song!
If you make a joke, at my expense?
I'm not sorry that I killed your mum!

He danced around the stage, twirled, threw in some soft shoe.

I wrote a script for Regulus,
Thought a genie
Might be fun!
The whole season was shit!
Was mine the worst of it?
And I thought, 'Well, at least that's done!'

He was really belting it now. Losing himself in it. Just plain losing it. As if there was anything left of him to lose.

And that might have been the end of it,
But your mum wrote that fucking song.
An anthem making fun of me!
I'm not sorry that I killed your mum.

Fucker started doing jazz hands.

Wah-wah-wah! Oh no!
Wah-wah-wah! Oh yes!

Wah-wah-wah!

So I killed your mum…
Took her trousers, not pants!
And I also took Roland Yates' bat when I had the chance!

He unzipped the duffle, pulled out the cricket bat to show
the audience. God knows what they musta been thinking.
He started dancing with it like a cane.

So I kill sometimes?
She killed my career! (Word play!)
Thought I had it made, then along you came to kill
My biggest break in thirty years!

So don't you hide out in the darkness!
I'm here to settle things for once and all!
You've got me dead to rights under these lights!
You've got the genie at your beck and call!

I think it's time we talked things out.
What's my motive? You really want to know!
You've got questions out your arse, no doubt!
Well, all you have to do is fucking show!

I was almost ready. Just needed another minute. Zipper was
tricky. Did I have another minute? Couldn't remember how long
the song was.

Mister Hinkle, sir, I must confess, it's been a lot of fun!

But coming soon, a great big boom!
I'm not sorry that I killed, sorry that I killed

Alfie Norton pounded his chest.

I'm not sorry that I killed, sorry that I killed,
I'm not sorry
    that I
       killed
         your
MUUUUUUUUUUUUUUM!!!

He spread his arms wide as he belted out that last note. Wiggled his fingers. Sang one last *'Wah-wah-wah! Wah-wah!'* Did a little shimmy. Sidestepped. Clapped his hands together. *'Not sorry that I killed your mum! Ha!'* Alfie dropped to one knee and grinned the biggest, maddest, and jankiest of smiles.

Held for applause, the crazy fuck.

No one applauded. Obviously. With the orchestra done, the auditorium was quiet as the depths of space. And from Alfie Norton's position, just as black.

He didn't see me, out there in the darkness, looking down on him from the upper balcony.

I stepped up onto the guardrail. Like in LA. So so stupid.

And I shouted, 'HEY, NORTON! YOUR FILK SUCKS!'

He heard me. Stood. Looked up, I think. So hard to tell. He looked so tiny down there. Tiny and blue and mad and twirling Roland Yates' cricket bat like a goddamn lightsaber.

He whispered into his mic for all the audience to hear.

'Welcome to your final chapter, Mister Hinkle.'

Almost.

Oh. And I probably shoulda mentioned. From the neck down, I was dressed in Nigel's big red-feathered parrot costume. The stagehand attached the final cable.

I spread my wings and jumped.

FIFTY-NINE

Back in chapter forty-seven, Nigel told me, 'It's not a question of if you're going to die, Patty, but how spectacularly you can go out!'

He was talking about being swung around the New Amsterdam Theater in his big red parrot costume. Which, as an audience member, was really thrilling to see. But as the person being swung, being flung, being launched through the theater faster than I could breathe?

It was absolutely terrifying.

I crashed into Alfie, knocked him down, rolled. He dropped the cricket bat. I hit the quick release on the parrot costume and the cables whipped away. Leapt for the bat. Expected to be racing Alfie, but he unzipped the duffle and pulled out a shiny, new croquet mallet.

'It was amusing to beat your mother to death with Yates' cricket bat,' he said, 'but my sport's always been croquet.'

We circled each other. I held the cricket bat out in front of me. A two-handed, defensive grip. He held the mallet in one hand. Let the head drag across the stage floor after him.

Blue flop sweat dripped down his forehead. Into his eyes. He didn't blink.

'You killed my mom,' I asked him, 'because of her song?'

He grunted. 'You might not believe this, boy, but before her little ditty, a lot of blokes quite liked that episode. *The Guardian* called it "a pleasant departure from a mostly maudlin second series." She poisoned them all against me!'

'And also,' I asked, 'you're a serial killer who's been murdering women and taking their trousers for, like, a hundred years?'

He sneered. 'These days, everybody needs a side hustle.'

The audience were out of their seats now and running for the exits. And the orchestra behind them. I didn't know it at the time, but the ushers were in touch with the bomb squad and were guiding everyone to safer locations inside the theater. Everything was wired to go off if anybody left.

I eyed Alfie's open duffle. Packed with explosives. I'd kinda hoped he'd been bluffing.

'If my mom's song hurt your career so badly,' I asked, 'why wait all these years to kill her?'

'Funny story.' It was not. 'I decided to move to Hollywood in the summer of '98. An attempt to revive my screenwriting career. And it occurred to me, as long as I was already in the country, I should hunt down your mother and bash her skull in with a croquet mallet. But, alas! I'd waited too long! Yates had died, and she'd disappeared.'

'She moved, like, four blocks.'

'It was harder to find people back then,' he grumbled. 'We didn't have the internet.'

'The internet definitely existed in 1998.'

He lunged forward. Took a swing at me. Two hands on the mallet. So much faster than I expected. I dropped down to one knee. Braced with the cricket bat. The two weapons collided with this tremendous clack. I gritted my teeth, shoved him back, stood, swung. He knocked my bat away. Swung again. He knocked my bat away.

'All right!' he shouted into his mic. 'I just wasn't very good at the internet back then!' I winced. His voice echoed through the speaker system. The whole theater shook.

I needed to calm him down. Lower his guard. Keep him talking. 'Then how'd you find her?' I asked.

'I was in New York last year to do some press for *Bridgerton* season two,' he explained. 'I met a woman at a cocktail party who told the most delightful story about an old employee who kept sending her joke emails.'

'Oh Evelyn,' I whispered.

'You'd be surprised what confidential information people will share for just the chance of meeting Regé-Jean Page.'

'But he wasn't even in season two!'

'It was February 2022,' Alfie deadpanned. 'A lot of people didn't know that yet.'

I swung. He dodged. He lunged. I parried.

Last of the crowd was outta the auditorium. It was just the two of us now.

'Any other questions,' he asked, 'before I bash your face in to match your dead mother's, then bring this entire fucking theater down on our heads?'

Shit. He wasn't planning on walking away from this. No third act for Alfie Norton.

All those people, huddling in the hallways. It was up to me.

'Yeah,' I said. 'At LaGuardia. I never figured out how you got in and outta that bathroom.'

'Well, if you don't know,' he said with a wild laugh, 'then I certainly can't tell you.' And he took another swing at me. Lazy. Easy to knock away. 'Is that really it, then? Is that really all you've got?'

'No!' I blurted. 'No, I, um…' I looked down at the cricket bat. That killed my mom. Killed her twice. Then back at Alfie. At his evil, withered face. At my mom's face, in my mind's eye. Broken and bloody. The zig-zag pattern of her shag carpet. No. Perfect. Young. Cast in green. Smiling at me. At peace.

I smiled back.

'Last thing,' I said. As calm as I've ever been. 'How were you gonna detonate all these explosives without a detonator switch?'

He laughed again. 'Haven't you guessed, my boy? By voice com—'

He didn't get to finish that sentence, because I bashed his ninety-four-year-old jaw and his fucking twitchy lip in. The crack of Roland Yates' bat echoed across the speaker system. Alfie's head spun. He spat blood and teeth and stumbled on his feet, and his mallet clattered to the floor.

'Actually, I did guess,' I said. And I hit him again, this time hard in the shoulder and I heard it break, definitely break, and he shrieked in pain, and I thought for sure that'd drop him, but he growled and he roared, this inhuman roar, and he pushed my bat aside and he barreled into me, knocked me down into the orchestra pit. I went crashing down into music stands, into abandoned instruments, with him on top of me.

Tried to brace myself during the fall. Was sure I was gonna break my back on a chair or crack my skull on a tuba or whatever, but it turns out that Nigel's parrot suit is ridiculously well-padded. I just kinda bounced where I landed, and then when Alfie fell onto me, I just rolled over and kept him pinned.

Took a sec to catch my breath. 'This is,' I conceded, 'kinda anticlimactic.'

He tried to say something back, to say the command to blow up the building I think, but the only noises that came out of his stupid broken mouth were incoherent and useless and pathetic.

I laid on top of him till the cops came.

'Good work!' said Detective Stuart as they hauled Alfie away in cuffs.

'I shouldn't have doubted you,' said Detective Bogdonavich.

And I saw that Lilly was there too, back near the lobby doors, so I excused myself to go talk to her. I had a little bit of a limp going, which I decided was pretty cool. 'Hey, babe!' I called. 'How's your day been?'

She met me halfway, tried to get me to sit, but I didn't really fit with the parrot suit on. So I wound up just awkwardly leaning against the arm of an aisle seat.

I handed her the bat. 'This belongs to Marv,' I said.

'You okay?' she asked.

I smiled, I think. I was pretty spent. 'I solved my mom's murder! You said I didn't have the temperament.'

She nodded. Squeezed my padded shoulder. I didn't really

feel it, but it was a nice gesture. 'Yes,' she said. 'You definitely really in real life actually did it, and not in a pretend made-up way.'

'Exactly,' I said. 'Can you help get me outta this thing?'

And she did. There was a hidden zipper in the back. I was achy and sore. It hurt stepping outta the thing, but I'd survived worse. Well, not really. This. This whole chapter and then stepping out of a parrot. This was the worst.

By the way, I was wearing a tuxedo under the parrot suit. Lilly was surprised.

'Oh yeah,' I said, and I reached into my pocket. Pulled out a little box, like the ones my pills come in. Except it wasn't that. I opened it up and showed it to her. Showed her the ring.

'I got you a thing,' I said. 'Do you like it?'

She smiled at me. Maybe cried just the tiniest tear from one eye. Wiped it away. Kissed me on the cheek. And said, 'That's nice, Pat. But maybe ask me in the real world. Not in your story.'

Which was good advice from fictional Lilly that I just wrote down.

I'll cap my pen in a second. Not my pen. Her pen. Real-her's pen. The good pen. The pen that writes upside down.

She'll be home from work soon. Real Lilly will. And I'll tell her how my day's been. How therapy's going. How Sasha's Kickstarter to save her shop is going. How Marv's AA is going. How just this morning, Lydia said that maybe she'd talk to me again someday probably.

I think about everything we've been through. How things are now. *How they should be.*

We've all got our shit. There's no silver bullet. No magic pill.

Oh! And I should tell Lilly about this tweet I read and how it's got me wondering if I'm maybe autistic too?

Probably I won't propose today. Probably I should buy a ring first. A real-life ring.

Real life's okay, I guess.

Never knowing who killed my mom?

Never knowing is okay.

We have stories for the rest.

When I was little, I had a nightlight. And when you wound it up, it'd play 'Twinkle Twinkle Little Star.' And every night, Mom would sing me to sleep to that song. Over and over, till the nightlight wound down.

And if I wasn't asleep, she'd stop anyway.

Wherever the nightlight stopped.

Sometimes mid-word.

And she'd shrug.

And she'd say,

'Sorry, Patty.

That's all y

ACKNOWLEDGEMENTS

I thought I knew my mom pretty well growing up. Understood her. She was a lot like me. Smart. Creative. Kind. Not super interested in doing chores. When I was a baby, she wrote a children's book, *The Unicorn Ring*, that never made it out of her drawer. Later, she got super into *Doctor Who*, took me to my first conventions, and helped run a fan club for the Third Doctor, Jon Pertwee.

They called the newsletter *The Pertwee Papers*.

So one difference between me and Patrick Hinkle is I got to see my mom young and full of passion. For a kid who was gifted but also frequently anxious and overwhelmed, that was everything. She was my example.

Do I wish I'd had an ADHD diagnosis when I was eight years old? Yeah. Heck, Mom might've benefitted from the same!

But I figured out how to get by watching my mom get by.

She's still alive, but age and health challenges compound. Her hearing, her energy levels, her memory. None of them are what they used to be.

I thought I knew my mom, but I have so many questions that I can never get answers to. There are so many stories that'll never be told. And not just *The Unicorn Ring*.

All I can do now is detective work.

Thank you, Mom. Also:

All my life, I've understood that my brain works different than a lot of other people's. For good and bad. The bad was mostly depression and anxiety, but also a lot of other little quirks that never seemed to add up to anything until I read an article by Nancy Kaffer for *The Detroit Free Press* where she talked about her ADHD diagnosis.

That article led me to an official diagnosis of my own, to treatment, and just a level of self-understanding, of self-awareness and self-acceptance, that I might never had reached otherwise.

My thanks to Ms. Kaffer. In no small part, this book is my effort to pay it forward.

My ADHD has historically made me a very, very slow writer, but I was able to write this novel in under eighteen months, a minor miracle, largely thanks to the regular encouragement and feedback from my weekly writing group, The Inkwells, including authors Sarah Beauchemin, Michelle Fogle, E.M. Hanzel, David Hoffer, Steven Nickell, Carol Pope, and Ruth Roberts. Thank you all!

And thanks as always to my editor, Dr. Victoria Barnes, who immediately got the assignment with this one and didn't blink twice when I told her that the punctuation was like that on purpose or that I was going to put all of the direct quotations in single quotes for… reasons?

I also need to thank my beta readers for their reflections and insights, including Karen and Elise from Bluesky and friends Jeff Furletti and Dylan Moulton from… Earth, I guess? And, of course, my wife Laura, the alpha of my betas.

Unless that's weird. That's weird.

Pretend I said a different thing.

And lastly, to my kiddo Sam, who is only nine as I write this and definitely hasn't alpha, beta, or omega-read this book yet, but who will someday hopefully pick it up off a shelf and connect with something herein.

Because, for all the stories that are never told, now and then we write some down. And hopefully that makes a difference.

Thank you.

ABOUT THE AUTHOR

Drew Melbourne is the neurodivergent geek author of *ArchEnemies* (2007) and the Percival Gynt books, *Conspiracy of Days* (2018) and *Inevitability of Fire* (2025).

Drew was born and raised in the Philadelphia suburbs, where he read a lot, played a lot of *Dungeons & Dragons*, and watched a lot of *Star Trek* and *Doctor Who*.

He graduated *magna cum laude* from the University of Pennsylvania with a degree in Creative Writing. If not for his ADHD, he presumably would've either majored in something more practical or written many, many more books by now.

After a couple of decades spent New Yorkering, Drew returned to the Philly suburbs where he now lives with his wife Laura, best kiddo Sam, and cats Elsa, Dancer, and (omg why am I not done listing cats yet?) Kitten McTalkerson.

You can find Drew online at <u>drewmelbourne.com</u>.

MAXIMALIST
EXISTENTIAL
SCIENCE-
FANTASY
ADVENTURE
COMEDY
IN THE
201ST
CENTURY

"LIKE POSTMODERN
DOUGLAS ADAMS"
- PUBLISHERS WEEKLY

drewmelbourne.com/PercivalGynt

HE WAS THE LOVE OF HER **LIFE**.

NOW SHE'S THE LOVE OF **THEIR** DEATH.

"STAY," SHE SAYS, as the life seeps from my body, as the night grows black and cold and indistinct. As I lay in her arms. As I breathe my last breaths. "Stay with me," she whispers.

As if I have that choice.

"You have to..." I wheeze. It's so hard to form words. I can feel the virus overtaking me. Killing me. Changing me. "You have to go. Run."

I'd shout at her if I could. Shove her. Say the most vile things to make her go. Do anything to save her. But I can't.

"I won't leave you," she says through heaving tears. She's not arguing with me. It's a statement of fact. And an apology.

I can feel them gathering, out there in the dark. The Dead. From the highway. Out of the woods. At the edges of the parking lot. And at the back of my skull. Closer. Closer.

A shambling inevitability.

"You have to keep going," I say. Haltingly. Each word's a struggle. Each word, as easily my last. "You'll be safe at your moms'."

She shakes her head, tries to wipe away her tears with the heel of her palm. She doesn't think she can make it alone. A hundred miles. But she can. She has to.

I shove my fingers into a bloody pocket. "Was gonna give you this there." Pull out the ring. Almost drop it. Fingers are going numb.

Such a tiny thing to represent something so huge. It was all I could afford.

She puts her hands around mine. And I feel her. Only her. See only her. My Jess. She's smiling and crying and she's filthy and wet with my blood and her hair is a mess and the left lens of her glasses is cracked and she loves poker and box wine and 90s rock and Venn diagrams and staying up all night playing Wii and cooking-though-she's-very-very-bad-at-it. And me, I think. And she would have picked a major next semester, if the world hadn't ended, if her faculty advisor hadn't tried to eat her face. Would have decided on the life she wanted, would have decided on me, would have said "yes" maybe, would have introduced me to her mothers finally. To her sister. To her dog Ruffles.

If the world hadn't ended.

She nods slowly. Reluctantly. Takes the ring from me. My arms slump. Slides it onto her finger. "I will," she says.

They're so close now. Just my burnt-out Volvo between them and us. Their moans. My God, the stench of them. But still they call to me.

She has to run. Make it inside the store at least. "As long as you wear that ring," I say, with the last of my strength, "I'm still with y-yuh-yuh—"

Can't quite form the last word. That thing in my head. Can't think. Voices. Incoherent. Hungry. Pain.

And something else.

Ancient.

    Alien.

       Malignant.

          Taking hold.

       I can't stay.

     Can't.

       Can't.

       Can't.

I STAND UP. Look down. On her. On me. What's left of me. My eyes roll back. No. *Its* eyes roll back. What's happening?

I look down at my hands, my own hands, at the ends of my arms. Not quite there. Like smoke in a rainstorm. And behind me, a bright light. And music. Joyous. Raucous.

So very, deeply inappropriate.

I turn back to her. That thing in her arms is waking. "That's not me," I try to tell her. But my words are muffled, like shouting through water. I cry and I swear and scream out as loud as I can, "That's. Not. Me!"

She sees what's happening. Starts to panic. Pulls away, scrambles backwards. It tries to speak. A halting, inhuman garble. Tries to reach for her. Slowly lumbers to its feet.

She stands, turns, nearly runs straight into the horde. Stumbles. Screams. Dodges a rotted grip.

"The other way!" I shout helplessly. Thank God, she remembers. She breaks for the store, forty feet across the gas station parking lot, and pushes her way inside.

A tiny bell jingles. The horde turn to follow.

And that thing. That thing that looks like me? It takes a step after her too. Slow. Uncertain of its footing. Then another. And it growls a long, low growl.

"No," I say. No. And without thinking, I grab the creature by the shoulder and I shout, "I SAID NO!"

It stops and turns its head to meet my gaze.

THE NEXT MOMENT I'm in the store with Jess. I don't understand what's happening. If that thing really saw me. How I jumped from one place to another. What I even am.

Jess was the religious one. I never believed in much of anything before her. But if people can turn into those things? Like something out of a bad horror movie?

Why not this?

Jess's toppling all the shelves. Dragging them in front of the door and windows. Good, Jess. But it'll never hold.

She's desperate, still sobbing through her work, with short staccato heaving breaths. Swearing irregularly. "You're doing a great job," I say uselessly.

I try to help her move one of the larger shelves, reach for it with my rain-smoke hands, but they slip through. Of course, they do.

"I'm dead," I say, just to hear the words. "I'm a ghost."

"Is there…?" Jess is looking around now. It's dark in here. Overcast outside. All we have is a sliver of moonlight. "Is there anyone in here?" she calls out.

Who is she talking to? Does she hear something I don't?

Outside, one of the Dead hurls itself against the glass. Then another. Then it's all of them as one. One creature with many bodies. And the glass is cracking.

Jess doesn't scream. Doesn't run. She's crouched, nervously gathering snacks off the floor and stuffing them into her purse. Good. No. Amazing. She's not just thinking about the next thirty seconds. She wants to live.

The glass shatters. The dead scramble over those toppled shelves with singular purpose:

To kill what lives.

It's getting darker inside. They're blocking out the

moonlight. Jess runs to the back of the store. She remembers seeing a door, but it's been swallowed by the darkness. She gropes along the walls.

They're inside with her now, staggering closer. Moaning. Growling. And the noises that aren't quite words. Like they're trying to tell her something, but can't.

She's found a door knob now. She's turning. Pulling. Is it locked?

They're so close now. Come on, Jess.

I have to do something.

Maybe. If that thing out there, the thing that used to be me, if it saw me? Felt me? Heard me?

"STOP!" I shout. I've placed myself between the horde and her. "STOP!" And they do. For this moment. Can't quite see them in the dark. They're just halos of moonlight. The suggestion of a tilted head. Inhuman whispers. "STOP!" I say again.

One of them advances before the rest, a dark and seething shape. It raises a gnarled, three-fingered hand towards me. Towards her? I don't flinch, even as it swipes its hand through my jaw. Ice cold.

It recoils. Hesitates. The whole horde murmurs in confusion.

Behind me, Jess has found the bolt. The door swings open, light rushes in, and Jess is racing out into the night.

"You won't have her," I say quietly. Firmly. But whatever momentary advantage I had over them is gone. Whatever element of surprise.

They bark and roar and clamor through me, like a rush of ice water, knocking me back, burning my insides.

And I scream.

A NOVELLA BY **PATRICK HINKLE**

drewmelbourne.com/GhostAndZombie

www.ingramcontent.com/pod-product-compliance
Lightning Source LLC
Chambersburg PA
CBHW031255120726
47906CB00003B/749